Everybody Ain't Your Friend

An Urban Romance Thriller

TANISHA STEWART

Everybody Ain't Your Friend: An Urban Romance Thriller
Copyright © 2021 Tanisha Stewart

Everybody Ain't Your Friend: An Urban Romance Thriller is a work of fiction. Any resemblance to events, locations, or persons living or dead is coincidental. No part of this book may be reproduced in any written, electronic, recording, or photocopying form without written permission of the author, Tanisha Stewart.

Books may be purchased in quantity and for special sales by contacting the publisher, Tanisha Stewart, at tanishastewart.author@gmail.com.

Cover Design: Carrie Bledsoe
Editing: indieink.net

First Edition
Published in the United States of America
by Tanisha Stewart

Dear Reader,

I hope you enjoy this urban romance thriller. Once you finish the story, I would love it if you left a review. Not sure what to say? This is fine – just comment on the characters, or your overall thoughts on the book.

Pressed for time? You can also just leave a star rating (1 = low; 5 = high). Either way, I would love to hear from you. I read all reviews left for my books and often use the feedback to improve future releases.

Lastly, if you would like to connect with me, feel free to join my reader's group, Tanisha Stewart Readers, on Facebook, or my email list at www.tanishastewartauthor.com/contact.

I look forward to hearing your thoughts and interacting with you!

Tanisha Stewart

Table of Contents

Everybody Ain't Your Friend

An Urban Romance Thriller

Chapter 1: Mia

There was one thing I could not stand.

I was hungry as hell and my ribs were touching. I went to get something to eat on my lunch break and wanted nothing more than to beast down on my meal. As I was eating, minding my own business, I felt eyes on me. I could not stand that shit.

Annoyed, I swallowed my bite and looked up to see him.

It was an older white dude with a buzz cut, staring all up in my face.

It was always the people who stared at you while you were eating that had the nerve to look disgusted at people who were sloppy eaters. Focus on your own plate instead of paying so much attention to mine.

I sat there and stared at him while he continued to sit there and stare at me.

He wasn't even eating his food. Just sitting there staring and shit.

Wearing a royal blue windbreaker jacket and some Pro-Ked sneakers. Who the fuck wore Pro-Ked sneakers?

I became furious.

He wanted a show? Okay, I was gonna give him a damn show.

I devoured my plate, not trying to be polite at all.

I was eating tacos, so of course it was gonna be messy as hell, but I didn't care. I had sauce dripping, meat dropping, and cheese all over my face, not to mention the sour cream.

Of course, I wasn't staring in a mirror so I couldn't see how disgusting I looked, but I was pretty sure it was ridiculous.

In response, he finally took a bite of his food, but he didn't take his eyes off me.

He was pissing me off, sitting there looking cool, calm, and collected while I was acting like an idiot.

Since I finished my tacos, I decided to confront him. I cleared my face with some wipes I kept in my purse and threw my container in the trash, then I made my way over to his table.

He wanted to be rude to me, so he was gonna learn today.

"Hey!" I said as I approached him. "Didn't anybody ever tell you not to stare in somebody's face while they are eating?"

"I'm sorry?" he responded in a neutral tone.

It pissed me off even more.

I opened my mouth to give him a full piece of my mind, then I saw the walking stick.

And the damn guide dog who was sitting right next to him.

I felt like a fool.

"Miss? Did you say something?" he asked, breaking me out of my stupor.

My entire face felt like it was on fire. "N-no..." I stammered. "I'm sorry, I thought you were watching me while I was eating."

His expression didn't change, but he did chuckle. "It's fine. I get that a lot."

"You do?" I felt my embarrassment wane slightly.

"Actually, no, but if it makes you feel better..."

That got a laugh out of me.

"I am so sorry," I repeated.

He shrugged. "It's cool. Sometimes people who are sighted are more blind than those with the disability." *Ouch, but I deserved it.* "How about I pay for your lunch?" I offered.

"How about I pay for yours?" His voice held a clear undertone, and that threw me for a loop.

"Huh?"

"Obviously, I can't see you, but you sound like a really beautiful woman. I'd love to take you out sometime."

I picked my jaw up from the floor.

At that moment, one of my huge, bouncy curls flipped over into my left eye, so I pulled it behind my ear. I had just gotten this style done by my homegirl Becky, who worked at a hair salon.

My hair never cooperated with me when I tried to do it, but when Becky put her hands on it, it was like she had a gift. If it wasn't for her, I would be sporting a botched attempt at slicked down baby hairs with a bun every day. Today, however, these curls were sitting right, and everywhere I strutted, they bounced in alignment with me.

My focus returned to the older white man who was hitting on me.

This man had to be at least twenty years my senior and was completely different from anyone I had ever been attracted to.

Still, I low key would have taken him up on his offer if it wasn't for one minor detail.

I smiled at him, though I knew he couldn't see me. "I certainly would go out with you if it were under different circumstances. Unfortunately, I'm happily taken."

"Damn," he grunted. "You're married?"

I laughed. "No, not married, but I have a boyfriend."

"So, I still have a chance?"

I laughed again. His ass was funny as hell. "Sorry, I don't think my boyfriend would appreciate it if I said yes."

He shrugged. "It didn't hurt to try."

"You have a good day, sir."

"Jeff. Sir's are old. I age like fine wine."

"Okay, I ain't mad atcha. Have a good day, Jeff. I'm Mia, by the way."

"Mia? Damn, now I know you're beautiful with a name like that."

My caramel skin definitely had to be blushing crimson now. I could not believe Jeff was really macking on me like this! I couldn't deny I liked it though.

"What do you say?" Jeff was saying. "I can still take your number down. We'll keep it on the low."

Jeff's ass was too pressed for me, but he was hilarious. We chuckled together, then I let him down lightly once again. "I must admit I am beautiful, but you'll find someone. Just keep your sense of humor."

"Okay, Mia. See you around."

I almost said, "You too," but I stopped myself.

"Ha!" he said, and we laughed together one more time before I went to pay for my meal.

The way The Cafeteria was set up, I could visit any area and place my order. The restaurant was only like ten minutes from my job, and they had a pizza station, a chicken station, a sandwich station, everything a person could think of, all in one building. Wherever I went I would tell them my name and they would put my order on a tab. My card would automatically be charged on my way out.

4

I told the lady at the cash register to put Jeff's order on my tab, too. It was the least I could do after a blunder like that.

I exited the building with a smile on my face. I couldn't wait to tell my boyfriend, Tray, about what happened. I whipped out my phone to do just that, then turned just in time to see a car racing toward me at an aggressive speed.

I jumped out of the way, but the car kept going until it was out of the parking lot.

"What the fuck?" I said, my heartrate subsiding now that I was out of danger. Did somebody really just try to run me over? Why?

After a few moments I calmed, reasoning that maybe the person was late getting back from their lunch break and didn't notice me.

"People need to be more careful." I shook my head.

As I was walking to my car, Jeff's words came back to my mind. *Sometimes people who are sighted are more blind than those with the disability.*

I had no idea why those words hit me at that moment, but they stuck with me.

"That was kind of deep," I said, then I got in my car and headed back to my job.

***

When I got home from work, I couldn't wait to tell my baby Tray about my day. I had meant to call him after I got back from my lunch but I ended up having a stack of claims on my desk to process, so I couldn't. "Bae!" I whined as I walked in the door, kicking off my heels. "I thought I told you not to let me wear these shoes anymore..."

5

My voice trailed off as I noticed Tray looking sullen sitting at the kitchen table.

"What's wrong?" I asked.

"Mia, I have to tell you something."

My heart dropped.

"What is it?" Tray was worrying me with this serious tone. Usually, he was goofy and playful like me.

I hope everyone is okay, I thought as I stared at him. His silence made me even more nervous. Then a tear appeared at the corner of his eye.

I gasped. "Oh my God, Tray! Baby, tell me what happened?"

He swallowed. "Mia, they lied to me."

My head snapped back. "Who? Who lied to you?"

He waited a beat, then responded.

"The people on the commercial. I didn't save nowhere near fifteen percent on my car insurance."

Then his facial expression changed into his signature grin.

He ducked as I swatted at him.

"Asshole! You really had me with that one."

He shrugged. "You got me last time, so I returned the favor."

Tray was referring to last week, when I called him up, pretending to be hysterical about somebody breaking into our apartment. He was so mad when he rushed in to see me sitting on the couch peacefully, reading a Lakisha Johnson book on my tablet and drinking a glass of red wine. Tray gave me a real *punishment* that night, and I enjoyed every moment of it.

I rolled my eyes. "Whatever."

"How was your day?" he asked, and I told him about work and my encounter with Jeff. He chuckled when I was finished. "Damn, sounds like I have some competition with this Jeff character."

I batted my lashes at him. "Oh, you jealous?"

"Nope."

I took a step closer to him. "You sure?"

He stood his ground, though I could tell he was getting hot because of the way I was looking at him. "Nope, my spot is solidified."

"Solidified, huh?" My gaze flickered downward. "Well, you're certainly solid. I can attest to that."

I grabbed him in my hand and gave him a gentle squeeze.

"Aw, come on, woman. Dinner before dessert."

I licked my lips and saw him changing his mind, then I reneged to get him back for his prank. "If you say so." I gave him a curt nod and walked toward the stairs leading to our bedroom.

"Wait! I was just playing..." his voice trailed after me.

I flipped him the bird as I continued up the steps.

***

By the time I finished my shower, Tray was done cooking. It wasn't much, just some Hamburger Helper, but he tried to spruce it up by adding onions and a few additional seasonings.

"Is this what I pay you for?" I joked, extending my loaded fork toward him.

"Whatever, woman. It was all I could manage with the way you left me."

I chuckled. "Hopefully next time you learn not to play like that."

"Psshht, my prank was nowhere near yours. You could have made me get into an accident!"

I felt bad when he said that. "True. Sorry, baby."

One of my curls broke free at that moment, and I smoothed it behind my ear.

"You are so sexy," Tray said, and I knew what that meant. His ass wanted me to give him another *payment* for my previous prank.

Shit, I wouldn't mind. Tray's lips and tongue did most of the work anyway.

We ate in silence for a few more moments, then Tray told me about his day at work. He worked at Walmart as a stocker. His supervisor was always getting on him about one thing or another.

"I'm so sick of that place." He sighed. "I can't wait til I finish school so I can get the hell out of there."

He was training to be a dental hygienist at one of our local community colleges. He was in his first year, but he planned to start looking for practices that had openings once he finished his next year. The school he was attending had a lot of intern opportunities, so he was hoping to score a position at one of them.

"You'll get there, baby." I smiled at him.

"Thank you, baby."

We finished our food, and I washed the dishes, then we went upstairs to our bedroom so we could binge a few episodes of *All American* before we went to sleep.

I woke up at some point later that evening to use the bathroom and saw that Tray was not in bed with me. Where is he?

I used the bathroom, then I was about to go downstairs to see if he was in the living room when he came back upstairs, his phone in his hand.

"What were you doing down there?" I asked, looking between his face and his phone.

"Nothing. Just got a call from my job asking if I could come in early today. I told them no."

He sounded like he was being honest, but his eyes told me he wasn't telling the truth. I pressed him.

"Why would you go downstairs to talk to them, though?"

"I didn't want to wake you." He was standing very still, like he really wanted me to believe him. I continued to stare at his face for clues.

"Tray..." I didn't know what to say. In our five years of being together, I never had to question Tray about anything. He was always so sweet, cool, charming, and attentive. This situation was throwing me for a loop.

Am I overreacting?

Before I could finish processing my thoughts, Tray took my hand.

"Mia, let's just go back to bed. I'm tired, and I know you are, too."

I didn't know what else to say, so I followed him.

Pretty soon, he was snoring peacefully, but every time I closed my eyes, my mind kept playing tricks on me.

He's hiding something.

No, he's not.

He lied to you...

No, Tray is a good man...

Finally, I couldn't take it anymore, so I crept over to his side of the bed, picked his phone up from his nightstand, and swiped the screen, punching in my birthday.

My heart filled with disappointment as the error message popped up.

He changed his passcode.

***

The next morning, I didn't know what to think.

After I saw Tray had changed his passcode, one part of me wanted to wake him up right then and there and demand to know what was going on, but another part of me told me I was overreacting.

Tray was my boo, my baby. We didn't have problems like this.

I had to be trippin.

I took some melatonin to help myself get to sleep, and when I woke up, Tray was gone. I looked at my phone and saw that he texted me.

Hey, baby. I tried to wake you, but you were sleeping hard. Made you some coffee and breakfast since last night's meal was such a disappointment.

He sent a winking emoji after that.

My mind was in overdrive. *See, Mia? Everything's fine. He's acting normal. Nothing is going on.*

I went downstairs and saw that Tray had indeed made me some breakfast. He left it in the microwave so it would stay warm. It was a ham and cheese omelet, some French toast, and he had even cut up some cantaloupe and strawberries and left them in the refrigerator.

I took the plate out of the microwave and the fruit from the fridge, then headed to the table.

My phone buzzed with another text. I swiped the screen, thinking it was Tray again, but it wasn't. *Better watch your back, bitch.*

It was from a weird looking email address. It had a bunch of letters and numbers and a foreign looking provider name.

"What the hell? How did this person get my number? And why text me from an email address?"

I didn't want to chance responding in case it was somebody who could steal my identity.

My mind flashed to yesterday. Almost getting run over by a car and receiving this random ass text message from an email address wasn't sitting right with me. I decided to let it go, however, and focus on my meal. Then I felt a draft. It sent a shiver down my spine. Where was the air coming from?

For a second, I freaked out. I went to grab our big butcher knife from the chopping block, then realized it wasn't there.

When I noticed that, I rushed to the sink to see if maybe Tray had used it without washing it, and it was in there.

My fear subsided. "Damn, Mia. Chill," I told myself. I still had to figure out where the draft came from though, since the front door and kitchen windows were closed.

I found out when I went to the back of our apartment, where our dining room was, and saw that our back door was ajar.

"What the hell? Why is Tray leaving the door open like this?"

My mind flashed to the night before. Did he go outside to talk to his job? It was a feasible idea, since he claimed he didn't want to wake me. But still, why would he leave the back door open?

I shook my head and wiggled my shoulders to get my mind off of that.

I closed and locked the back door, then went back to the kitchen after checking the rest of the downstairs rooms to make sure no one was in the house.

After checking the downstairs, my paranoia returned and I grabbed the butcher knife out of the sink to go check the upstairs too, cursing myself for not bringing it with me when I checked the downstairs.

Chill, Mia. You're bugging, my mind told me.

No one was upstairs.

I finally relaxed.

When I got back to the kitchen, I threw the butcher knife back into the sink, then sat down to eat my breakfast. I sent Tray a text, cussing him out for scaring me half to death by leaving the back door open.

I didn't leave it open, he responded.

Whatever, I shot back. I still wasn't sure how to feel about Tray's alleged phone call to his job last night. Part of me told me I was bugging, but another part felt like he wasn't being truthful.

As soon as I finished washing my dishes, I heard the doorbell ring.

"Hey!" I said when I opened it to see my two besties, Loryn and Becky standing there.

Becky was looking glamourous as usual, with a honey blond wig that had a wavy bang in the front. Her hair went down to her shoulders and went perfectly with her cinnamon-colored skin tone, and when she batted her lashes, I saw that they were popping too.

"Hey, girl! What's wrong with you?" Loryn asked.

Loryn was looking cute as well, with her black box braids with beads interwoven in them. Loryn had the lightest skin of our trio, and me and Becky often pissed her off by calling her a light bright.

"What's wrong?" Loryn repeated.

Damn, I guess I wasn't good at hiding my emotions. I didn't want to get into my suspicions about Tray with my girls, however. Especially since they were probably nothing. *Probably isn't definitely,* my mind told me, but I ignored it.

"Nothing."

"What do you plan to do on your day off?" Becky asked.

"Apparently, spend time with you broads." I smirked for emphasis, hoping that would make Loryn think I was okay. I didn't want to mention the Tray situation just yet, in case I really was trippin.

"Tuh, whateva," Loryn said, flipping her box braids over her shoulder.

Becky was already making her way to the couch. She flipped on the flat screen TV, and started searching through the guide for a show or movie.

Loryn and I followed and plopped down, with me sitting in the middle of them.

"Girl, these walls are bare as fuck," Loryn said, looking around my living room.

It was true. My walls were bare except a huge portrait of me and Tray that was hanging above the TV.

"Damn," Becky said as she nodded. "We need to get you together."

"Fuck y'all," I said with a chuckle.

"At least a rug or something," Loryn said, now looking down at our hardwood floors.

Becky chimed in again. "Y'all dusty asses done been in this apartment for how long again? And all you got in your living room is a couch, a loveseat, and a TV."

"Whatever." I rolled my eyes, though their comments were starting to get to me a little. "We got the glass tables, which helps."

Loryn looked at my round glass table, which was in the middle of the living room, then the two glass end tables on either side of the couch and love seat. Her eyes lit up. "Oh, you know what, Mia? We could get you some

13

of those fancy glass bowls and fill them with potpourri. That would make your living room pop for real."

Becky's eyes widened too, catching the vision. "Right! You know Billie's is having a sale this weekend, right? They got all kinds of little figurines and paintings and stuff. We could really get this place looking good, girl."

My heart warmed with gratefulness for my friends. I wasn't much of a decorator. My mom had been getting on me about doing something to our living room and kitchen ever since Tray and I moved in four years ago.

Tray never seemed to notice or care about decorating, and I didn't have creative insight, so I just let it go. "Thanks ladies," I said. "We can definitely head to Billie's this weekend."

We started watching *Real Housewives of Atlanta*.

Chapter 2: Mia

After Loryn, Becky, and I binged a few *Real Housewives* episodes, we got bored and decided to go out for lunch and pedicures. Loryn suggested we hit up Billie's to pick up a few things since we were going to be out, but me and Becky decided against it. I didn't have any money til the end of the week when I would get paid, and Becky said she only had a couple of hours to spare before she had a special appointment at the salon.

I thought of Tray the entire time we were out chilling, even though I was trying to play it off.

When I finally got back home, I had a few moments to myself, so I decided to do some yoga. I was still very much a beginner, but I enjoyed all the stretching.

Tray liked to joke about me becoming so limber...

My eyes welled up for the third time that day.

The first time Loryn spotted it immediately, but I told her it was the spicy pepper I had just tasted. The second time no one noticed because I was sitting in the backseat as Loryn was riding shotgun and Becky was driving. They were yapping so much about hitting the club this weekend after we finished our shopping at Billie's that they didn't care to look back at me.

I didn't know what I was going to do without my man if the truth came out that something was going on.

Not that I needed a man, but...

I prayed he wasn't cheating and that there was some other explanation for all of this, but why would he change the passcode to his phone? Why'd he go all the way downstairs to make a phone call in the middle of the night?

The proof is in the pudding, Mia.

I shook myself out of my thoughts.

I heard Tray enter our apartment just as I was headed into the shower to prepare for bed. Our place had an upstairs and a downstairs, with the bedrooms and full bathroom upstairs, and the kitchen, dining room, living room, and half bath downstairs.

Tray called out to me, but I ignored him, continuing my nightly routine, except at a much earlier time of day. I knew I was being dramatic, getting ready for bed when it was barely past five o'clock, but I couldn't help it. All this was blindsiding me.

I stayed under the water until my skin became wrinkly.

After that, I headed downstairs to face my doom. My mind had gone back and forth so many times while I was in the shower that I felt like my head was going to explode.

I wasn't letting the night go by without a serious conversation.

I fought back my tears as I made my way down the carpeted steps to our living room. The living room had hardwood floors, but they were looking extra gleamy today for some reason. "What the hell...?"

I had barely finished my sentence when Tray came bounding into the room from the kitchen. He was wearing black ankle socks, but he was rushing so fast that he slipped and fell backward, busting his ass in the process as a small box flew out of his hand.

I broke out of character and burst into laughter at the sight.

"Tray, what the fuck are you doing?"

My eyes swept up and down his body as I fought to catch my breath. Tray was shirtless, with black silk shorts on and those black ankle socks. "Why are you walking around half naked?"

"Mmm, my neck, my back..." Tray fake moaned like he was really hurt. "I'm suing, woman!"

I walked over to help him up, but almost slipped myself because it looked like oil or something on the floor. "What's going on?"

I noticed Tray also had oil on his chest.

He shot me a sheepish look before grabbing my hand to get up. "I was trying to get all sexy and glistening for you."

I wrinkled my nose, though I wanted to laugh again. "So, you rubbed yourself down with baby oil?"

He smirked as he stared down at me from his now standing position. "I knew you liked my abs, so I was trying to take advantage of the moment, but then the bottle slipped and I guess I didn't get it all when I wiped it up."

I shook my head at his silliness.

"Why are you in your pajamas?" he asked, wrinkling his nose.

My heart panged as I thought of the fact that funny times like this might be over soon.

I searched his eyes for a second, then asked him a question. "What moment were you trying to take advantage of?"

Tray looked distracted for a second, then he snapped out of it.

"Oh, shit! Where is it?" He patted the sides of his shorts, but they didn't have pockets. Then his eyes scanned the room until both of us caught the small box that was strewn near the front door.

My entire body went hot, then cold as I clapped my hand over my mouth. My eyes grew as wide as saucers as Tray went over to retrieve the box, then came back to me, grinning.

"Tray!" was all I could manage as he got down on one knee.

"Don't start calling my name just yet, woman. There will be plenty of time for that later."

He winked, then opened the small box and revealed the most beautiful diamond encrusted ring I had ever seen in my life.

When Tray looked back up at me again, there were tears in his eyes. "Mia, I have loved you since the first moment I saw you. You're the sweetest, sexiest, most intelligent woman I have ever met. I couldn't see my life without you, so I wanted to know, would you be my wife?"

I was overcome with emotion.

"Tray, I thought you cheated!" My voice croaked as I spoke.

"Cheated?" A puzzled expression crossed his face, then he looked worried.

"Last night when you went downstairs."

He blinked. "Oh, no. Mia, I got up to use the bathroom and I checked my notifications. I saw that I had an email from the jeweler, and he was saying the ring might not come in on time. I planned to pick it up today because I wanted to propose on the day that we first met. I went downstairs to go on my laptop to find the name of the company who was shipping the ring. I was gonna call as soon as they opened and cuss they ass out, but when I got up for work, the owner called me and said he was able to push it through."

I felt like an idiot as realization dawned.

"Wow... Tray, this is so beautiful."

He grinned again. "I know, right? It's a cubic, but it looks like the real thing."

He dodged me as I swatted him.

"Always playing!" I fake whined.

"You know you like it, but anyway, woman, my knee is growing numb. Are you mine forever, or what?"

I pursed my lips. "I guess so."

He cocked his head. "You guess so? Shit, let me see if I can get my money back."

"Boy, if you don't give me my damn ring!"

We both grew serious again as Tray took the ring out of the box and slipped it on my finger. It fit perfectly.

"How'd you know the right size?"

"I measured you in your sleep," he deadpanned.

I rolled my eyes and he chuckled.

"Nah, I'm just playing. I asked your mom."

"Hmph."

After Tray got back up from kneeling, we went into the kitchen where we shared a candlelit dinner. He had gotten some food from Ruth's Chris, trying to be fancy.

I couldn't front. I was totally surprised that he proposed.

My eyes welled with tears for the umpteenth time that day as I stared into Tray's eyes. Here I was, worried for a whole day that my man was cheating, but in reality, he was planning the sweetest proposal ever.

I didn't remember the date of the first time we met, but apparently Tray did. He was always thoughtful like that, despite his silliness.

I eyed my ring once again. It was so beautiful; even better than I ever imagined my engagement ring would be. I looked back up and saw Tray staring at me. The intensity in his eyes was so deep, it was overwhelming.

I had to take a sip of my wine to calm myself.

"Tray, this whole evening is beautiful."

He smiled. "Not as beautiful as you."

After we finished dinner, Tray showered to get all the baby oil off his chest, and when he reentered our bedroom, I knew it was on.

I had quickly changed into some lingerie while he was in the bathroom to surprise him, since he had surprised me so much with this proposal.

I still couldn't believe it.

This was surreal.

I was sitting up in bed reading a book on my tablet when Tray stood in the doorway with a seductive expression on his face.

I put my tablet on the nightstand, then toyed with him. "What happened to the silk shorts?"

His gaze swept up and down my scantily clad body, then he made his way over to me as I stood to meet him.

Tray stared into my eyes without answering my question.

He wrapped his arms around my waist, and I wrapped mine around his neck. I looked up to meet his gaze yet again, then rested my head on his right shoulder. He was smelling like the Dove Men's body wash I bought him.

"Mmmm," I murmured.

I felt his lips on my neck, then my heat rose.

"Tray..."

My voice trailed off as he moved from my neck to my lips, indicating that he wanted us to talk with our bodies rather than words.

We shared a passionate, soulful kiss that steadily increased with intensity.

Soon, sexy lace top was long forgotten and my bare breasts were exposed. The only things separating us were his boxers and my panties. I pulled down his boxers, then slid my panties down and stepped out of them.

I imagined our wedding night. Would it be as sensual as this? Or even more so?

"What are you thinking about?" Tray asked, speaking for the first time since our encounter began.

"Our wedding night," I answered truthfully.

"Oh?"

I nodded.

"How about we give ourselves a little preview?"

I swallowed as he stepped closer, then we made love like we never had before.

***

Loryn and Becky were hanging at Becky's house the next day after work. I had an easy load that day, processing property damage claims. I decided to bust up in the apartment to surprise their asses.

"Ding ding, bitches!" I waltzed into the living room, swirling my hand around in a silly fashion so they could see my ring.

"Bitch!" said Loryn, looking shocked.

Becky's eyes were wide, too. "Tray proposed?"

I beamed. "Yup. Girl, he did it last night, and it was so magical."

I stared at my friends, waiting for them to urge me to continue, but they didn't. After a few seconds passed, I spoke again. "Well, damn. Y'all don't want to hear how it happened?"

21

Loryn snapped out of it first. "Yeah, definitely. It's just that me and Becky were talking about some news that I had."

"What news?" I demanded, my hand on my hip.

Her lower lip quivered. "Mia, I'm pregnant."

My jaw dropped. This was definitely not what I was expecting to hear. "Who, what, when... what the hell?"

Loryn didn't even have a man. As far as I knew, she wasn't dealing with anybody, either. How was she pregnant?

My eyes shot to Becky. Her eyes told me she just found out about this today, too.

I picked my jaw up from the floor. "Girl, who is the damn baby daddy? Let's start with that!"

Becky stared at Loryn, too. It was clear that was probably what she was asking Loryn before I burst in the door using my spare key.

Loryn gave one to both of us in case of emergency.

Loryn's eyes shifted. "I don't want to talk about that."

Becky gave her a side eye. "I know it wasn't Jermaine's dusty ass."

"Ew, I hope not either." Loryn had been messing with this dude named Jermaine in the past, but she said she was done with him after he took her on a date to McDonald's, then asked her to loan him two hundred dollars the next day.

Loryn was really going to keep messing with him after that, but me and Becky convinced her not to.

Our instruction didn't work, because here we were.

Becky and I tried a few more times to get Loryn to tell us if Jermaine was the father, but she refused to talk about it, which let me know he was.

"It doesn't matter who the father is," Loryn kept saying. "I just need to figure out how I'm going to rearrange my life to include a damn baby."

Becky blinked when Loryn said that. "Well damn, bitch. Ain't a baby supposed to be a blessing?"

"It is, when the father is..." Loryn's eyes clouded.

My heart went out to my friend. "Girl, what is Jermaine's number. Call his ass right now, so we can set him straight."

Becky cut in. "Right. He's going to have to get a job or something, because he is not leaving you out here like this. You didn't make this baby yourself."

Loryn just stared straight ahead.

Then she changed the subject back to how she was going to manage daycare expenses.

"Damn, you thinking of daycare already?" Becky asked. "You still got a while nine months to worry about that, girl."

"I still think we should call Jermaine," I said, but Loryn ignored me.

I decided to let it go. Loryn would call him on her own time. Pregnancy was no joke. She was probably still processing the news herself, so to have Jermaine try to scream on her or something right now would be too much. I knew she would be fine though. Loryn had a good head on her shoulders, despite her poor choice in men.

After leaving Loryn's house, I called Becky so we could debrief about the conversation via Bluetooth on our way to our respective homes.

"Ugh, I don't know what we gonna do with Loryn's silly ass," I started.

"Don't be too hard on her, Mia. You know she never picks the right niggas."

23

"Yeah, but when he asked her for two hundred dollars after meeting her less than a week prior, she shouldn't have needed us to tell her that was a red flag. I can't believe she still fucked him."

"Shit, maybe she needed the D. Girl, it's been a while for both of us. You're the only one with a man."

My eyes caught the glint of my ring on the steering wheel as I continued to drive.

Becky's comment reminded me of the fact that I never got to tell her and Loryn the full story of how Tray proposed.

That low key hurt, but whatever. Maybe I could tell them another day.

I shook myself from that thought. "Anyway, his ass better step up to the plate and see if they can make it work or something."

"Right. Or at least pay child support or something."

Becky and I chatted a bit more about Loryn and Jermaine, then she got to her house, so we hung up. I pulled up to me and Tray's apartment a few minutes later.

"Damn, Loryn," I said, shaking my head at my friend's situation before getting out of the car.

Tray was going to be out late tonight, chilling with his boys Trevor and Anthony, so I would most likely be reading some books on my tablet until I got tired.

I wondered if Tray told his boys yet that we were getting married?

I stared at my ring, then I started reminiscing.

I remembered the day me and Tray met five years ago. I was out with Becky and Loryn during sundress season, but I was wearing a wifebeater, sweatpants, and Adidas slides with black socks because I had my period.

Loryn and Becky were all dolled up, so they started talking shit about me looking like a butch.

"Fuck both of y'all," I said. "I bet I could still pull a sexy nigga, sweatpants and all."

"Yeah?" Becky asked with mischief in her eyes. She nodded across the food court in the mall to the most beautiful man I ever laid eyes on. He was wearing a black fitted Boston cap, a black t shirt, a gold chain, a wristwatch, some jean shorts and black Jordans.

I wanted to fuck him on sight.

I was suddenly pissed I was looking crazy.

Becky's voice snapped me out of my stupor. "I dare you to go up to the one in the black shirt and ask him for his number."

"Girl, I am not doing that."

"Why not?" Loryn said, eyeing the dude as well. "He is hella fine."

"Yes, he is, but I'm clearly not looking my best today."

"I thought you said you could pull any nigga you wanted?" Becky asked, her eyes still on him. "When he turns you down, tell him to take my number instead."

"Shit, or mine," Loryn added.

"Bitch, I saw him first," Becky said.

I sat in my seat, wondering if I was really ready to embarrass myself off of this dare.

"You gonna do it?" Becky asked.

I sighed. "Whatever, Becky, but next time you gotta do whatever I dare without reneging."

Becky flipped her blond-colored tresses behind her shoulder. "Deal."

I made a funny face at her, then walked toward Mr. Sexy. Why the hell did I agree to this? "Whatever," I said under my breath. I tried to rehearse what I would say to him and how I would play it off when he turned me down so I could give him Becky's number. "I swear this bitch owes me," I said before I stopped in front of his table.

Mr. Black shirt looked up at me, along with his boys, Mr. Green shirt, who was also kind of sexy, and Mr. White shirt, who probably had a nice personality.

"How you doing?" I asked. I forced a smile.

He looked me up and down. "Good... How are you?"

Mr. Green shirt was already smirking and covering his face to keep from laughing as he put two and two together.

I didn't let his chuckles break my stride as I focused on Mr. Black shirt. "Do I know you from somewhere? 'Cause you been running through my mind all day." I tried to be cool by saying that line, but from the way Mr. White shirt burst out laughing, I knew I had fucked it all the way up.

Mr. Black shirt smiled and my heart fluttered. Damn, this was a bad idea.

"Was that a pick up line?" he asked.

I tried to save face as I prepared for my doom. "Maybe. If you want it to be."

He looked me up and down as Mr. Green shirt and Mr. White shirt stared. "Well shit. I'll try anything once. What's your number?"

My jaw dropped as he pulled out his phone.

His boys were looking back and forth between us as he asked me my name so he could add it to his contacts.

"Mia," I said.

He licked his lips. "Damn, that's a beautiful name. I'm Tray, by the way. But let me ask you something, Miss Mia... If you and I started talking, would this be your first time?"

My brows furrowed. First time? What did he mean by that? Then it dawned on me: Tray must think I'm a lesbian! I chuckled, not breaking my character.

"No, it wouldn't," I responded, but I left it at that.

I couldn't believe he actually wanted to talk to me.

Part of me wanted to look back at Becky and Loryn, but another part of me didn't want him to think I was trying to play him. There was something about Tray that drew me in.

Later on, as we got to know each other, Tray told me he felt the same way about me.

He thought I was a lesbian or at least bisexual because of the way I was dressed, but when he found out I wasn't through our conversations, our relationship bloomed. We started spending every weekend together, then every weekend turned into a few times a week, then every other day, then we went ahead and got an apartment.

And now, we were getting married...

I wiped a tear that slid down my cheek as my ring glistened yet again.

Chapter 3: Mia

I could not wait to start planning me and Tray's wedding. I already decided I wanted a white dress. Becky and Loryn would be my bridesmaids, of course. I wasn't going to bother making one of them a maid of honor because I knew whichever one I didn't pick would never let me live it down.

I spent the first hour of my job at Miletti Insurance Claims Center sneaking and looking up different styles for the wedding party. It wasn't hard to keep my online activity a secret because we processed mostly property claims for water damage, fires, and the like. Part of my job was to look up comparable items to what clients lost to price match, and much of the time that included things like clothes and shoes.

I had a heavy caseload today, but my head was in the clouds.

Just as I was looking at tuxes for Tray, he texted me.

I'm about to quit this fucking job.

I snorted in response, causing Evelin, one of my coworkers, to turn and stare at me.

"My bad. Tray just texted me."

She nodded, but gave me a stank look before turning back.

Fuck was her problem?

I wasn't going to say anything to her, though. I focused on my phone screen. We were allowed to text while we were on the floor as long as we kept our errors to a minimum and produced a steady number of finished cases.

You'll be fine, Bae, I responded. *Just go to the spot for a minute.*

Tray and his coworkers had a designated spot they went to in the store whenever the managers were pissing them off. It was in a back room near the stock area.

Can't. Ricardo is on my ass.

Ricardo was Tray's supervisor. He was the reason Tray sent me this same text every few days telling me he was quitting.

Can you take your fifteen?

Tray and his coworkers were allowed two fifteen-minute breaks and one thirty-minute lunch.

Good idea. Clocking out now.

My worry for him dissipated when I saw that message. I knew all Tray needed was some fresh air and a couple of minutes away from Ricardo so he could calm down.

He would likely be outside with his boy, Trevor, who wore the white shirt the first day we met, and his boy Anthony, who was wearing the green shirt. Trevor's job was to keep track of the shopping carts in the parking lot, and Anthony worked at the sneaker spot that was right next to the Walmart Trevor and Tray worked at.

I texted him a half hour later just to make sure he was good.

He didn't text back, so I assumed he calmed down.

***

Finally, it was time for lunch. I headed to The Cafeteria to grab some tacos, since they had been calling my name from this morning. Since The Cafeteria was located in the downtown area of our city, it had business from all over. Sometimes it was packed to capacity, but they had outside seating too, so I usually found at least

29

one empty table. If not, I would just take my meals back to my job to eat. Today, they weren't that full, thank God.

I called Becky since she usually took her break around the same time as me. Becky was a hairdresser at Heavenly Tresses, a salon owned by this girl we went to high school with named Monica.

"Hey, girl," I said, grabbing up my tray and heading straight to the taco station.

My eyes caught Jeff sitting a few tables away from the spot I saw him at last time. He didn't have his dog with him, but he had his walking stick.

"Hey," Becky replied. She sounded a little upset.

"What's wrong with you?"

I briefly considered saying hi to Jeff, but decided against it. Maybe I would catch him on my way out if he wasn't gone already.

"Nothing. I'm just sick of Monica's bougie ass."

"What she do?"

"What doesn't she do? She just raised our booth rent again, which isn't necessarily a problem because I work my ass off, but then she instituted a new rule that we can't double book clients anymore."

My jaw dropped.

Becky always had tons of women and men coming to her for braids, styles, color, and having their locs retwisted. She did outstanding work, plus she was fast, so everyone wanted a seat in her chair.

"Why did she do that?"

"Because of Bria's slow ass. Remember how I told you she always tries to compete with me? Her ass started double booking because she saw how much money I was making, but she didn't realize that I have a technique to my shit. She had a client go off on her in front of everybody for having her wait over an hour for service. After that, Monica made the new rule."

"Damn, that's fucked up, Becky. Can you and Monica work something out since you never had that problem?"

"I already tried, Mia. She's not hearing me."

I paused. I wanted to say I kind of understood where Monica was coming from because she was most likely trying to be fair by giving everybody the same rules, but I knew Becky would be pissed at that.

"Girl, I don't know why you don't go get your own salon, anyway," I said instead. "You have the skills and the clientele."

Becky thought about it for a moment.

"I don't want to deal with even more competition. You see how Shanay always be trying to sabotage Monica since she got her salon."

Shanay was Monica's best friend when we were in high school. They both went to school for business and cosmetology after we graduated. Their original plan was to open up a place together. Shanay ended up getting pregnant and dropping out of school, so Monica got a head start.

Once Shanay's baby was old enough to go to kindergarten, she went back to school. She was going to work at Monica's salon, but they had a falling out, which led to her opening her own. She had been doing underhanded stuff ever since to try to mess up Monica's reputation.

Becky continued. "Anyway, let me go back in here. I got a client coming in ten minutes."

"Oh, I thought you were taking your lunch?" I looked at my watch to check the time again. Becky always took her lunch the same time as me.

"It's a special appointment."

"Oh, okay. I'll talk to you later. Want to get up after work? We can chill at my place."

"Yeah, call Loryn too because I need some drinks."

"Right... wait, she's pregnant."

"Damn, I forgot that quick."

"More for us."

"Shit. I'll see you."

I hung up with Becky and ordered my tacos. I glanced over to where Jeff had been sitting, but he was gone.

***

Becky didn't waste no time. Her ass got to me and Tray's apartment before I did.

"Damn, girl!" I said as I exited my vehicle clutching a brown paper bag containing two bottles of Stella Rosa.

She held up her own paper bag in response. She was already standing outside her car when I pulled up. "We bout to turn up."

We walked to the front door and I opened it. The way our apartment was set up, the front door opened directly into the living room. The kitchen was off to the side, the half bath was between the kitchen and living room, and the dining room was down a short hallway in the back.

"Ugh..." Becky said as she plopped down on our couch. "Why don't y'all get a rug in here or something? Don't these floors be cold when you walk barefoot?"

For some reason, that triggered my memory of Tray busting his ass sliding across the floor in those black ankle socks. I burst out laughing, then my laughter turned to the threat of tears.

"What?" Becky asked.

I calmed because I was getting a little emotional over the fact that nobody outside my mother heard the story of how Tray proposed. I was probably being dramatic, but didn't friends usually want to hear the story of how it happened? Yet, neither Becky nor Loryn asked me.

I shrugged to get myself away from that thought. Both of my friends were going through stuff right now. Loryn was about to be a single mother because we all knew Jermaine's ass wasn't stepping up to no plate, and Becky was dealing with drama at her job. It was easy to miss stuff in other people's lives when you had problems in your own.

At least that's what I was telling myself for now.

"Um... hello? Mia?" Becky was waving to get my attention.

"Huh? What you say?"

She gave me a side eye. "Nothing. Girl, just get some glasses or something. I need to unwind."

I wordlessly went to the kitchen to grab the glasses. Becky was already opening one of the bottles. When I returned, she filled a glass for each of us, then we sat back on the couch to continue our conversation.

"Girl, what you think Loryn bout to do with Jermaine's ass?" Becky asked.

"I have no idea. We told her he was a scrub, but she was being hardheaded."

"I mean, her job pays enough for her to take care of herself, but still. I wouldn't want to have a baby by a nigga that ain't gonna do shit for me."

"I agree, but if she never wants to listen to nobody, what could we possibly say?"

Becky took a few sips of her wine. I tasted mine, and it was hitting.

"Anyway, I was thinking about what you said, Mia. I think I am gonna see about getting my own salon."

My heart swelled with pride for my friend. "Get it, girl! I know you can do it!"

Becky took another sip, then nodded. "Thank you, girl. But where would I even start?"

I thought for a second. "You could do research on the best locations, then you could see about a business license. I'm not sure the exact process for salons, but I know with your skillset, you could definitely do it and start out with an advantage."

Becky had downed half her glass and was already pouring more wine by the time I finished my speech.

I could tell she was nervous at the thought of having her own business.

"Well if you think I could do it, I guess I need to believe in myself too," she finally said.

I grabbed the wine and poured some more for myself. "Shit, let's drink to that."

Two bottles later, Tray walked into the apartment followed by Loryn. Loryn was supposed to meet us when we arrived, but she never showed up. Becky and I had called her phone a few times, but she didn't answer.

Becky was a little tipsy since she had done most of the drinking. "Finally!" she said to Loryn. "Bitch, you done missed most of the party not answering your phone."

I nodded as I stared at Tray.

My eyes shifted to Loryn as well. "Girl, where you been all day? Did you have an appointment or something?"

Loryn gave me a stank look in response.

"What?" I asked. "Why you got an attitude?"

She cleared her throat. "Tray and I have an announcement."

I blinked and Becky cocked her head. We both spoke at the same time. "Announcement?"

Becky and I shared a glance, then turned our attention to Loryn and Tray, who were standing a little too closely for my liking. Tray looked guilty for some reason, while Loryn's expression was smug.

She turned to Tray. "You want to tell her? Or should I?"

Now I was standing. "Tell me what, Loryn? What does she need to tell me, Tray?" I felt heat rising within me and it wasn't good.

Becky stood as well, assessing what was about to go down.

Tray didn't say anything, so Loryn got impatient. She turned back to me.

"Long story short, I been fucking your man. He's mine now."

"Bitch, what?"

Before anybody could answer my question, I was on Loryn's ass. I was trying to do some serious damage, but it was halted by Becky and Tray holding me back.

"She's pregnant, Mia. You gotta calm down," Becky said.

I wrenched myself from their grasp, but I didn't rush Loryn again.

Becky shot Loryn a look, and if looks could kill, Loryn would be gone.

"I can't believe you did this!" I said to Loryn. "You're supposed to be my best fucking friend!"

I turned to Tray. "Why the fuck would you propose if you didn't mean it?"

Tray finally spoke. "Baby, it's not even like that."

"What the hell do you mean it's not even like that, Tray? You're fucking my best friend. What else is there to explain?"

Something else dawned on me. "Don't tell me you are the one who got her pregnant, Tray."

Tray's Adam's apple bobbed up and down, then he looked away.

I lost it again. I lunged at Loryn, but Becky grabbed me.

"It's not worth it!" she said, but I wasn't hearing her.

I was looking at Tray and seeing my man standing in front of my best friend like she was his woman instead of me.

"I can't fucking believe you," I said to him. "Get out of my house."

"Gladly," Loryn said before Tray could respond. "Get your things, Tray. You can come to my place."

Just like that, my entire world was shattered.

I didn't know what to think or what to do.

Becky stayed there with me as Tray threw some clothes and toiletries in a bag and left with Loryn.

"I can't believe that dirty bitch," she kept saying over and over again.

I didn't respond. My mind was on Tray and how he just up and left me like that without even giving an explanation.

Tray

I knew I fucked up, but I hoped Mia would hear me out when we had a chance to talk. I never meant for this to happen. I didn't even like Loryn like that. I mean, she was cool as Mia's friend, but that was always it as far as I was concerned.

I would never hurt Mia like that.

Basically, what happened was I got drunk one night after a fight me and Mia had. I was out with my boys, Trevor and Anthony. We hit the club to blow off some steam and ran into Becky and Loryn while we were there.

At first, I thought it was strange they were out without Mia 'cause I figured they would be at our apartment with her talking shit about me, or at least she would be there with them, as she told me she would be earlier.

At first, I felt bad, being out at the club, while my girl clearly stayed home, but I was still pissed at her, so I said fuck it and stayed.

Me, Trevor, and Anthony were turning the fuck up.

There were mad bitches in there, and Trevor and Anthony were both ladies' men so they were mingling. I joined in, too, but I wasn't really trying to mess with nobody 'cause my mind was on Mia.

Then I did something stupid.

Anthony proposed a shot game with the chicks we were chilling with and I joined in. I saw right through their bullshit. They were trying to get those girls drunk to go home with them, but I ain't say shit 'cause I was in my feelings.

I participated in the game and got more drunk than anybody but I tried not to show it.

I went to the bathroom and next thing I knew Anthony and Trevor's asses were gone.

Trevor must have forgotten I rode with him to the club, while Anthony had met us there. He was so thirsty for the chick he was talking to that he left me.

I called him but he didn't answer his phone.

I walked out of the club to see if he was still in the parking lot and ran into Loryn and Becky. They asked if I needed a ride, and I said yes. I hopped in Loryn's whip because she lived closer.

On the way to me and Mia's apartment, she told me she had to pee, so we stopped at her spot. I had to piss too, so I went inside with her. When we got in there, I was kind of wobbly, so she offered me a glass of water.

I took it, but I was so tired I fell asleep right there on her couch.

The next morning, I woke up butt ass naked in Loryn's bed with her crying next to me.

I looked over at her and she was naked, too. She told me we had sex.

"What?" I had said, not believing my eyes or ears. "What the hell you mean we had sex, Loryn?"

She sniffled. "Tray, I'm so sorry. I didn't mean it. I was drunk, but then I was feeling lonely. You were so out of it, you kept trying to kiss on me and kept calling me Mia. I kept trying to tell you I wasn't her, but you didn't get it. Then it started feeling good so I just gave in."

"You just gave in? What the fuck?"

That was singlehandedly the dumbest shit I ever heard, but my mind was swimming.

"Yo, you can't never breathe a word about this to Mia. I swear, Loryn."

She got quiet.

"I know. It would break her."

Fast forward to today, I was at work and Ricardo was on my back. I went to take my fifteen-minute break to chill with Trevor and Anthony. While we were outside, Loryn pulled up to us all of a sudden saying she wanted to talk to me.

I hopped in the passenger seat, praying that she wasn't about to be on no bullshit after popping up on my job like this, and that was when she dropped the bomb that she was pregnant.

She told me she would meet me after I got off work so we could talk about it further. I spent the rest of the day worried as fuck, then when I got off, she was parked next to my car in the lot.

The plan was for us to tell Mia and apologize, but Loryn flipped the script when we got to the house. I wasn't expecting her to lie and say we had been having an ongoing affair.

I swore it was just that one time.

When we got outside, I cussed her ass out and went to crash at Anthony's house. Loryn was on some other shit with that.

I wanted to go back in to talk to Mia, but I could tell from her response that her mind wasn't straight.

Neither was mine.

I didn't know what to do.

Chapter 4: Mia

All I could think about was Tray.

I had a lot of questions for him, but I wasn't sure if I was ready to hear the answers. My best friend, Tray? Really?

Out of all the women he could have slept with, he chose Loryn?

He'd been calling and texting me since last night saying he wanted to talk, but I couldn't speak to him yet.

It was definitely over, but I eventually I would need some type of closure to see why he did it.

Did it even matter why he did it if the damage was already done?

I didn't understand why he would go through all that trouble to propose to me if he knew he was sleeping with Loryn the entire time, and got her pregnant.

What the fuck was I to him?

Apparently, our relationship didn't mean shit.

I sat there on the couch, lost in my thoughts, dark circles under my eyes because I couldn't sleep the whole night before. I had called out of work this morning because I just couldn't do it today.

I had gotten another bottle of Stella Rose from the corner store after eating a quick breakfast. I wasn't really hungry, but I knew I would pay for it later if I drank on an empty stomach.

My phone buzzed with a text. At first, I thought it was Tray, but when I read the screen, I saw it was Becky.

Hey girl, how you feeling?

I'll be okay, I texted back, then put my phone face down on the couch next to me and turned up the TV.

I thanked God for Becky, for real. Becky held me down last night. I was speechless after Tray and Loryn left together, and Becky immediately went into Momma Bear mode.

"Don't even worry about her, Mia," she said. "We got something for Loryn's ass as soon as she drops this baby."

"It's not even worth it, Becky," I responded. When I first heard the news, I was ready to slice Loryn's fucking throat, but at that point, I felt like all my strength was gone. Tray had just proposed and got me all excited, just to break my heart like this.

I was so defeated. Deflated.

Becky assessed me. "I'm spending the night with you. No way I'm leaving you alone after something like this."

I sniffled. "Thank you, girl."

"You know I got you. I can't believe Tray would do something like this, but you know what? It's better you found out before y'all got married than after."

I knew she was just trying to help, but it didn't.

"Right," I still said, trying to breathe more slowly so the pain that was filling up my heart wouldn't shatter it completely.

Becky stayed the whole night as she promised, then told me she would stop in again after work. I had no idea how she could still go to work after staying up all night with me, but apparently, she had energy for days.

Still lost in my thoughts, I barely noticed my phone buzzing again with a text. I swiped my screen, and it was from that weird email address again, except this time it wasn't a written text, it was a voice clip.

It was only seven seconds long, so I decided to play it. A distorted voice came through my speaker. It sounded like a computerized and muffled version of Arnold Schwarzenegger. *"Got what you deserved, bitch. Game time."*

I didn't have time to play with Loryn's ass. She already had my man. What more did she want?

I finished my bottle of Stella Rose and I could feel my mind swimming. Still, it didn't take away from my depressing thoughts.

My mind drifted to Tray, yet again.

I remembered the day after we became official.

I had gone over Becky's house eager to share my good news. Once I told my friends, both of their jaws dropped.

"Are you serious?" Loryn had said, but there was a hint of sadness in her eyes due to the fact that she had just broken up with her latest boyfriend, Darnell.

"Get it, girl," Becky had said with a smile.

We went out to eat and I ended up getting severe food poisoning.

Even though our relationship was brand new, Tray actually came to the hospital while the doctors were assessing me with flowers and a teddy bear.

"Oh, wow, you didn't have to!" I said to him.

He smiled from ear to ear. "I just needed an excuse to see your beautiful face."

"Thank you so much, Tray." I inhaled the soothing scent of the flowers.

He sat there with me for a few hours, then followed me home when they discharged me.

I was out of commission for a few days, but Tray came to visit me every day, bringing me Gatorade and water, and everything he could think of to make me comfortable.

He was so sweet.

What went wrong?

I heard the phrase a thousand times that niggas ain't shit, but I really thought I had a good one.

Guess not.

Chapter 5: Mia

Two days later...

Fuck that shit.

I might not have been ready to talk to Tray yet, but I was more than ready to talk to Loryn.

Right when I was about to go to her name in my contacts, however, Becky called me.

"Hey," she said.

"Hey."

"What are you doing?"

"About to call this bitch. She owes me some answers."

"Shit, I know that's right. Put her ass on three-way."

Becky didn't need to tell me twice. I called Loryn up immediately, ready to give her a piece of my mind.

"Hello?" she answered on the first ring like she was expecting me.

"Loryn, what the fuck is wrong with you?" Becky cut in before I had a chance to speak.

Loryn chuckled. "Oh, so both of y'all bitches want to try to pop shit?"

"Where is this attitude coming from?" I chimed in. "We were cool just days ago, and now you're acting like you don't even know me."

Loryn blew out a breath. "Look, it's not my fault you don't know how to catch a hint. I stopped fucking with you a long time ago. Now that I got what I wanted, there's no more need for pretending."

I couldn't believe my ears.

Becky cut in again.

"What are you saying, Loryn? You been plotting on Tray the whole time they were together?"

Loryn chuckled. "There wasn't much plotting needed if you ask me. He came willingly."

"See, that's the shit that's gonna get you in trouble," I warned.

Loryn mocked me. "Was that a threat? Don't try me, bitch. I press charges."

"Funny how you mention pressing charges when you're the one harassing me."

"Harassing you how?"

"Playing on my phone with random ass numbers. Shit is not cute, bitch."

"Nobody has time to play on the phone with you. I have my man now. I got what I need."

Becky cut in. "The only reason you're breathing right now is because you're pregnant with your hoe ass."

"Becky, shut the fuck up. Your weak ass wasn't about to do shit, pregnant or not."

"Excuse me?"

I cut back in. "Look, this conversation is unproductive. I called you to find out how you could do something like that to me, and apparently, I got my answer. In your eyes, we were never friends."

Loryn wasted no time agreeing. "Yup, that's right. Now, if you'll excuse me, my man is on his way to our home to discuss how we're going to take care of our child. I'll send y'all an invitation to the wedding once we set the date."

She emphasized all the words in her statements that involved putting her and Tray together, and it got under my skin.

"Bitch, you—" Before I could finish my sentence, Loryn's line disconnected.

"Arrrggghhh!" I screamed, then I threw my phone so hard that it shattered, pieces flying everywhere on the hardwood floor.

Chapter 6: Mia

I could barely get out of bed these days. It had been a month, and I felt like I was losing my mind.

I buckled down and got a new phone last week.

Tray had been coming over and trying to talk to me, but he couldn't get in because I changed the locks. He would bang on the door and plead for me to let him in, but I just couldn't face him.

I knew I was only prolonging the inevitable, but I'd never had my heart broken like this.

Becky had been coming by every couple of days after work.

She was my rock, along with my mom.

My mom kept telling me to hear Tray's side of the story, but Becky was against it.

"I respect your mom and everything, Mia, but what they did was crazy. You didn't deserve that."

I didn't know which one I should listen to, so I'd just been numb.

All I did was work, eat, sleep, and shit.

A knock on my front door shook me out of my thoughts.

I knew it was Tray because of his pattern. Tray's hand was obviously stronger than Becky's, so his knocks were a little harder.

I ignored it for five minutes before he left, just like he did every other time.

Then my phone buzzed with a call from a private number.

I had blocked Tray's number as soon as I got my new phone, because I would be damned before I inconvenienced myself rather than him by giving out a new phone number to all of the bill companies and friends or family who needed it, but somehow, I knew this private number was him.

I decided I had time today.

"What do you want?" I answered through gritted teeth.

"Mia, why didn't you open the door? Baby, I need to talk to you."

"You don't need to say shit, Tray. Loryn told me the whole story."

Tray sighed. "Mia, I swear it's nothing like what you think."

A tear rolled down my cheek. I wasn't ready for this. I lied to myself.

"What do I think, Tray? Besides the fact that you slept with my best friend and got her pregnant?"

"That's what I'm trying to tell you. It wasn't—"

"And how long have you been seeing her, huh? According to Loryn, it's been a minute."

"No, the fuck it hasn't. I don't know why she's lying like this."

"What do you mean?"

"It only happened one time, Mia, and I was drunk."

I took my phone away from my ear and stared at the screen as if Tray could see me. I knew he didn't think I was that stupid.

"What, do all cheaters follow the same handbook or something? Why do y'all all come with that *it was only one time* or *I was drunk* bullshit?"

"I'm not lying. That's what it was."

"You know what? Fuck you, Tray. Save your explanation."

I hung up.

Tray

She wasn't hearing me.

After everything we had been through together I figured she would at least give me the benefit of doubt.

Mia was over there acting like I was some ain't shit nigga when I had been holding her down since day one.

You know what? Fuck that.

My sadness turned to anger just that quick.

I called her ass back.

"Hello?" she answered with attitude, probably expecting me to continue begging like I had been doing for the past month and some change.

My next words let her know I wasn't playing anymore. "How dare you sit there and not even bother to listen when I try to explain to you what happened."

"Excuse me?"

"You heard me, Mia. I been coming to that house every single day trying to talk to you. I called your phone over a thousand times in the past month. You blocked my number and won't even talk to me, but I'm the piece of shit? Bitch, look in a mirror."

I knew I fucked up when I said the word *bitch*. I hadn't meant for it to come out that way. That was a problem I'd had since childhood, flying off the handle and saying shit I didn't mean before I had time to think. I opened my mouth to apologize, but Mia was already responding.

"Bitch? Nigga, who the fuck you think you calling a bitch?"

I tried to fix it.

"I didn't mean to call you a bitch, but Mia how can you act like our relationship meant nothing to you?"

"Ain't that the pot calling the kettle black? And I still got your bitch, nigga."

This conversation was not at all going how I had hoped. I tried again. I was glad my boy Anthony wasn't home. I had been staying with him since Mia kicked me out. Things had been cool so far, but I knew I was cramping his style, since he liked to have women over often. I tried my best to stay out of his way. I sighed. "Mia, I've been trying to explain to you that what you think is not how it went down!"

I heard her huffing and puffing and sucking her teeth on the other line.

She was pissing me off with her attitude. After everything we had been through, I would at least have expected her to hear me out.

"Are you hearing me?" I asked.

"You better fucking take that bass out your mouth, boy."

"I wasn't yelling."

"No, you weren't, but your tone is way too harsh for someone who is guilty of cheating. You need to come correct, or don't come at all."

I was done. She clearly didn't give a damn what I had to say. "You know what? I don't even know why I tried so hard to get back with you. If this is what you want, I don't need to explain shit to you. It's over."

"Bye then."

I heard her sniffle before she hung up, but I didn't say anything.

I was pissed off for a second, but then I wanted to call her again.

I did, but she didn't answer.

I called again, but she still didn't answer.

Then Anthony came home. Sooner or later, I was gonna have to make arrangements to get my own place or something since it was clear Mia didn't want to act like an adult.

Calm down, Tray, I told myself. *Remember, she thinks you were cheating with Loryn.*

At that moment I felt guilty all over again.

Somehow, I had to find a way to have a civil conversation with Mia.

Chapter 7: Mia

Becky met me at The Cafeteria to get a bite to eat and so I could tell her the latest about Tray. We went to the taco station, then sat at the last empty table.

Before I could open my mouth, Jeff walked up and sat a few seats over from us. He had his stick and his dog today.

Clearly, he didn't notice we were trying to have a private conversation, but all the other tables had people sitting at them, so there wasn't anywhere else for me and Becky to go.

"Girl, so tell me what happened," she said.

I glanced at Jeff before I spoke.

"He called me from a private number and I finally answered."

Jeff perked up from his roast beef sandwich.

"Mia? Is that you?"

Becky's eyes shot to mine. I shrugged.

"Yeah, it's me. How are you?"

"I'm good. Better now, though. How have you been?"

I had yet to tell Becky about my first encounter with Jeff where I embarrassed the hell out of myself, then he tried to talk to me.

"Not good, unfortunately," I said, so he would let me and Becky talk in peace. "I'm going through a breakup, so I was just telling my friend about it."

"Damn, that quick? I knew I had charm." Jeff smiled.

Becky was watching our interaction with a smirk on her face.

I didn't know how to respond to Jeff's last comment, but apparently, I didn't have to because I became distracted by who showed up to The Cafeteria next.

Tray made his way over to our table with a determined look in his eyes.

"Ugh, I don't have time for this shit," I said under my breath as he walked up to us.

"Mia, can I talk to you?" He looked so eager, I wanted to give in, but the bitch in me wouldn't allow it.

"No, you may not."

Jeff jumped in again. "Is this the loser? Back off, buddy. You had your chance."

Tray blinked at Jeff. "Who the fuck are you?"

"Leave him alone," I said to Tray. "That's Jeff."

I knew Tray would know who I was talking about since I told him about the situation.

Becky was all ears at this point.

Tray turned his attention back to me. "Mia, I need to talk to you."

"You already said everything you needed to say. Leave me alone so I can eat my lunch in peace."

"Mia..." he pleaded with his eyes.

"You heard the lady. Step aside so she can get with a real man."

Tray didn't enjoy Jeff's sense of humor.

"Yo, this really has no concern to you, my dude. I'm talking to my woman, and I would appreciate it if you left us alone."

"I'm not your woman," I clapped back.

Tray stared at me.

I could tell he wanted to say something else, but he decided against it.

"Okay then. If that's how you feel."

He walked away, and my heart went with him.

Jeff snorted. "What a sucker. You don't need him, baby girl. Whenever you're ready, hit my line."

He proceeded to take a card out of his wallet and slide it across the table toward me.

Then he nodded and got up. "I'll let you ladies continue your conversation in peace." He grabbed his sandwich and stick, exiting the cafeteria, the bottoms of his sneakers lighting up the entire way. His dog followed.

I remembered having those light up sneakers when I was a kid. If my heart wasn't broken over Tray, I would have probably laughed at seeing Jeff sport them.

When he was out of earshot, Becky looked at me like she didn't know where to start.

"Girl...what the fuck was that?"

I filled Becky in on who Jeff was and everything that went down with Tray before finishing my food and saying goodbye to her so I could make it back to work on time.

When I got back to my job from my lunch break there was a note on my desk from my supervisor, Jessica. *Mia, please come see me.*

I thought that was strange. Usually, Jessica would just send me an email or something. I wondered what this was about.

I clocked in on my computer, then pushed my chair in and went to Jessica's office. She was engrossed in her computer screen when I walked in, so she didn't notice me.

I lightly rapped on her open door.

Her head popped up. "Hey!" Her expression and tone were neutral.

"Hey," I said, walking in. "What's going on?"

She sighed. "Can you close the door, please?" I obeyed, then turned back to face her.

"Listen..." she began as if it was hard for her to find her words. "I've had a few complaints from our anonymous system that you've been talking on your phone while you were on the floor, and some complaints also said you've been eating at your desk."

I blinked. What the hell? Although our job allowed us to text on the floor, talking was a no-no since it was supposed to be a quiet space. Food was also a no-no because people got carried away years back and there was a rodent infestation.

"I have not been doing either of those, Jessica," I said.

She sighed. "I figured you weren't, but do you mind if I search your desk just for protocol? And also, could you please keep your phone away for a few weeks?"

I didn't know how I felt about Jessica searching through my desk, but I hadn't been eating there, so I guessed it wouldn't cause too much harm.

"That's fine," I said.

We walked over to my desk. I noticed that Evelin, my coworker, perked up when she saw me with Jessica.

"Hey, Jess!" she said.

"Hey," Jessica said, barely looking at her. I went to my desk drawer and used my key to open it. When I did, my eyes popped open and my jaw dropped.

There was a half-eaten, moldy looking Pop-Tart in there, along with pieces of gum stuck to the bottom of the drawer. In addition to that, there were empty chip bags, and some tiny black ants were crawling all over everything. I wanted to puke.

"Jessica, I swear," I said, but before I could finish my sentence, Evelin was up and out of her seat.

"What is it? Oh, my God, that's gross!" She looked at me in disgust. "Why would you stick gum in the bottom of the drawer?"

Jessica looked at me. My entire face was red.

"I swear, this was not me."

Jessica looked pissed that she would have to put in a maintenance request. "Please move to cubicle twenty-eight for the remainder of your shift, Mia. Once you're ready to clock out, come see me."

I swallowed. I wasn't sure how to handle this situation. Someone else clearly had gotten access to my desk to do this, but I had no idea how. Only employees and their supervisors had keys to their desk drawers.

Maybe I left my key one day? I wracked my brains. That was certainly possible, but if that was true, why would someone randomly choose my desk to put all that junk in? I barely ever used my drawer. I never needed to since I didn't bring anything inside the building but my purse and cell phone, both of which I always carried with me.

Somebody clearly set me up, and I figured I already knew who.

Chapter 8: Mia

Once I finished getting my writeup from Jessica over some shit I didn't do, I went straight for Evelin's ass in the parking lot.

"Hey!" I said, catching up to her.

She looked at me like she was afraid. "What is it, Mia?"

"Did you put that stuff in my desk?"

Evelin cocked her head back. "What stuff?"

"You know what I'm talking about, Evelin. All that food stuff."

She gave me a confused look. "Why would I do that? Plus, how? I don't have the key, remember?"

"But I could have left it on my desk when I went to the bathroom or something."

She shook her head. "Look, Mia, I don't appreciate you coming to me accusing me of something just to get the attention off yourself. You messed up fair and square. That has nothing to do with me."

Something wasn't right about her ass. Me and Evelin were always cool until about a month or so ago. I had no idea why she was being all stiff suddenly.

"Whatever, Evelin. Just stay away from my desk, okay? And I know it was you who sent those anonymous complaints, too."

Before I walked away from her, I swore I saw a smirk on her face, but there wasn't anything I could do about it.

When I got home, I was contemplating calling Tray.

I knew it was probably stupid as hell, but I loved him, and despite the fact that it had been thirty-nine days, I still felt like this entire situation came out of left field.

Then, I noticed that something was off.

The dishwasher was on in the kitchen.

Tray and I never used our dishwasher because neither of us were used to having one growing up. How could it possibly be on?

I crept over to it, like I expected it to blow up or something. Everything else in the kitchen appeared to be in order, except the dishwasher.

I opened the cabinets and saw that all the plates and cups had been removed. Next, I opened one of the drawers and saw that the utensils were gone too.

Then the machine signaled to let me know it was done.

I took a deep breath, afraid to open it. I didn't know if it was all the horror movies I'd watched in the past or what, but I felt like I'd open it and see a dead cat or something.

Finally, I willed myself to just do it.

I pressed the handle and whipped the door open before I could change my mind again.

The only thing inside were the dishes that were previously in my cabinet and drawer.

"What the..." my voice trailed off, then I jumped and shrieked when my phone buzzed on the kitchen table with a text message.

This damn apartment was going to give me a heart attack, sooner or later.

I looked at the notification, and it was that random email address again. *Take better care of home, bitch.*

Whoever this was, was starting to piss me off. How dare they come in my house? My body grew hot. I wanted to email their ass back, but I decided against it.

"Should I call the police, or what?" I asked myself. The obvious answer was yes, but what was I going to tell the police? Someone came in my house and washed the dishes?

I was not making a fool out of myself today.

I called my mother. "Mommy," I said when she answered.

"What's up, girl?"

"Can I stay with you tonight? Being in this apartment alone is scary."

"Tonight?" she repeated. "Um... yeah, I guess so."

I cocked my head like she could see me. "What do you mean, you guess so?"

She paused before responding. "Nothing, girl. Come on."

Now my mind was playing tricks on me about my mother. Why was she acting funny? Maybe she wasn't. Maybe it was all in my head.

I hung up with my mom and immediately got a call from a private number.

I wondered who it was. Tray had called me private before, but I did just get that message from the crazy person. Maybe they finally wanted to talk.

I moved to answer it, but the ring had run out.

A few moments later, I got a voicemail notification.

I swiped my screen to listen to it. It was Tray.

"Mia, I really need to talk to you..."

He sounded so lost and so sad, I wanted to give in.

If Tray was pushing up on me like he had been, there was no way Loryn had been telling the truth about them planning to stay together.

Maybe Tray was telling the truth. Maybe I should have given him another chance.

We all made mistakes, right?

I decided to talk it over with Becky to see what she said. I was in the middle of packing my bag to go sleep at my mom's house, so I put her on speaker.

I could barely finish my opening sentence before she was cutting me off. "Girl, I know you are not about to let that nigga play you."

"Becky, I can't help it! We were together for five years! I can't just get over him that quick."

"Well, you need to. I'm not trying to see you get hurt again when it seems like you are finally starting to come out of your shell."

I knew Becky was only trying to help me, but at the same time, I felt like she didn't understand.

I hung up with Becky, then went to my mom's house.

"Mommy," I whined when I walked in. "I want to talk to Tray."

She looked at me with her hand on her hip. "Then talk to him! Everybody makes mistakes, honey."

She walked toward the kitchen, and I followed. My mouth watered as soon as I saw that she had made baked chicken, green beans, and yellow rice, and she had already fixed me a plate.

I sat down and my mother sat across from me in front of her plate.

I bowed my head as she said Grace, then I re-started the conversation.

"But what if he does it again?"

Mom answered after taking a bite of her chicken and swallowing. "Then you leave him for good. Either way, the decision is up to you, but like I always tell you, I wish I had given your father another chance."

My dad had cheated on my mom when they were going through problems right after I was born. He begged and pleaded for her forgiveness, but my mom wasn't having it. A couple of years later, he married someone else, then my mom was filled with regret.

She said she felt like as long as he was single, her mind told her the door was open and she could walk through it whenever she wanted to. Especially since he tried to talk to her almost every time he came to get me, but when his advances stopped and my dad got married, her chance to make it right with him was over.

But still...

"Ma, me and Tray don't have a child, though."

"So? It doesn't mean you two aren't in love."

"You would really want me to go back to a man that cheated on me?"

"It's not about what I want. It's about what you want. You're young. This is your time to take your chances and make mistakes. It could be that he is sincere or it could be that he's not. You know Tray better than anyone else. What does your heart tell you?"

That was the million-dollar question.

I was so troubled after that conversation that I got down on my knees and prayed.

"God, please show me what I should do. I love him, but I don't want to get hurt again."

***

The next morning, I woke up to a notification on my phone.

That bitch, Loryn, had tagged me in a picture of her and Tray at an ultrasound appointment. There were two pictures in the post: one of her and Tray, and one of the sonogram photo.

I was disgusted. This bitch was really trying me.
I didn't know why I hadn't blocked her ass already.
I studied Tray's face. He looked annoyed, like he
didn't want her to take the picture.
Or maybe my mind was playing tricks on me.
Or maybe it wasn't.
I felt like a damn fool.
I decided to push Loryn and Tray to the back of my
mind and focus on work.
I forced myself out of bed, though I really didn't feel
like going now, especially since I was dealing with
bullshit there too. My mind went to the Evelin situation
and I contemplated calling out.
I decided against it, however, when I remembered
that I had already called out within the past two months.
The company had a two-call-out per ninety days
policy. I had called out the day after Tray and Loryn
made their announcement. I wanted to save my other
one in case I really needed it.
I took my shower to get ready, then was pissed when
I saw that the shirt I had packed had a stain on it.
I had taken it from my drawer and didn't remember
it being stained before.
"Whatever." I sucked my teeth, then headed home.
My mom was already gone. She liked to run errands in
the mornings and go for a jog with the other ladies in the
neighborhood, so I locked up her house before leaving.
I picked out a different shirt and hightailed it to
work.
When I got there, however, there were security
guards waiting for me along with Jessica.
"Mia, please come to my office."
I wordlessly followed her, still not over my
embarrassment from the previous day. The maintenance

guy was shooting me dirty looks the entire time he cleaned my desk drawer. Having to scrape that gum off the bottom of it had to be annoying as hell, so I didn't blame him, regardless of the fact that I didn't do it.

"What is this about?" I asked when we walked into the office and the security guards closed the door.

"Are you and Evelin having problems?" she asked, her face etched with concern.

I wasn't sure how to answer that question. "We had a discussion yesterday, if that's what you're talking about," I said finally.

"In the parking lot after work?"

I paused. "Yeah... why?"

Jessica sighed. "Mia, Evelin said someone pushed her down the concrete steps that led to the lower-level parking lot after her shift. She said it happened right after your argument with her. Would you happen to know anything about that?"

I couldn't believe my ears. This shit was getting out of hand. "Someone pushed her? Is she okay?"

Jessica nodded. "She's okay, but she said you were upset with her and accused her of trying to sabotage your job. She said you walked away, then when she was going to her car on the lower level, the incident happened."

Both of the security guards were staring at me like they believed I was guilty. Suddenly, I felt like the back of my shirt was sticking to me or something. I was sweating like a motherfucker. I prayed these people were not about to fire me, or worse, try to press charges or something. "Jessica, I have no idea who might have pushed Evelin. I'm sorry this happened to her, but it wasn't me."

One of the guards cut in. "There aren't any cameras in that area where Evelin was assaulted, so we have no way to prove it, but we would still like to take a written statement from you."

I filled out my written statement, then the security officers stood by the door until I walked out to go to my cubicle. Jessica didn't say another word to me.

I shot glances at my coworkers after sitting down. None of them looked like they knew what was going on, so I guessed there weren't rumors going around about me or anything.

Still, I spent the rest of the day worried that my time with the company was soon coming to an end. Why was Evelin doing this, though? No way in hell had I pushed her. I had walked straight to my car after we talked and that was it. I didn't understand.

By the end of my shift, my mind was back on Tray and Loryn.

I headed to the grocery store to get some ice cream.

Chocolate would help me clear my mind.

As I browsed the many selections of chocolate ice cream, I saw someone approach me out of the corner of my eye.

"Hey," he said.

I turned and looked, and my breath caught in my throat.

I had no idea who he was, but this man was fine as hell.

He was tall, mocha colored, with hazel eyes and lashes for days.

My eyes traveled to his full lips, then his thick, muscular neck, just as he cleared his throat. I became transfixed by his Adam's apple, then I blushed as my mind caught up to the fact that he was trying to get my attention.

"Hey," I said.

He flashed me a pearly white smile. "I'm Noland. What's your name, pretty lady?"

I became flustered. "Oh, it's Mia." I felt hot and cold all over for some reason.

"Mia, huh? Having trouble picking an ice cream?"

"What?"

He nodded toward the freezers. "You looked like you were deep in thought."

I snapped out of it.

"Right. I just needed something soothing."

He was silent.

Then I felt slightly embarrassed. *Soothing, Mia?*

Noland opened the freezer and picked up a carton of the chocolate fudge ice cream. "Something tells me this is what you need."

I blinked. The chocolate fudge ice cream was the exact one I was thinking of.

"Thank you." I took it from him.

"Glad to be of assistance." He smiled again.

I couldn't help but to return the gesture.

Noland continued. "So, you got a man?"

That snapped me back to reality.

"Yes... I mean, no."

His forehead creased in confusion.

"I'm getting over a breakup."

"Oh, I understand." He looked slightly disappointed. "Maybe I can help ease the process." Something about the way he said that was sexy as hell.

Suddenly I wanted Noland to help ease the process, and a few other things.

It had been forty days since I last had sex, and a girl was hurting.

But I wasn't about to be jumping from bed to bed like that.

I opened my mouth to turn him down, but he gently grabbed my phone that was in my hand.

I gasped, and he quickly handed it back. "Oh, my bad. I should have asked before just taking it, but do you mind if I put my number in your phone? Maybe if you're feeling up to it, we could talk later?"

This man had too much sex appeal for me.

My panties were getting wet just by the smoothness of his voice.

"Sure," I squeaked before I could stop myself. I tapped in my passcode, then handed Noland the phone.

He entered his contact info, then handed the phone back to me.

"Oh, so it really is Noland, with a D?" I asked, reading his name.

He smirked. "Yup, With a D." He looked me up and down and licked his lips before walking away.

I was in deep trouble.

Somehow Noland just came in and swept me up off my feet.

"Get your horny ass home," I breathed, then made my way to the cashier's aisle to make my purchase.

Chapter 9: Mia

I couldn't front, I low key wanted to call Noland. I just kept chickening out.

Part of me screamed *rebound*, but another part of me was saying that if I was really supposedly done with Tray, it might have made sense to cut my losses and give Noland a fair chance.

It had been two days since he gave me his number.

I was sitting on my couch, watching TV and thinking about Noland.

I didn't want to wait too long to reach out because he might have forgotten about me, but at the same time...

Becky called my phone, shaking me from my thoughts.

"Hello?"

"Girl, what you doing?"

"Thinking about this dude I met."

"Dude you met?" she sounded surprised. "What dude? When?"

"The other day at the grocery store. I went to get some ice cream, and he approached me. We started talking and I let him put his number in my phone, but now I'm scared to call him."

"What he look like?"

"Becky!"

"I need details, honey. If we doing this, I need to make sure he's an upgrade."

I described Noland's looks to Becky.

"Hell yes," she said when I finished. "I give my full approval."

I chuckled. "Bitch, you haven't even seen him yet."

"I don't need to. You had me when you mentioned his hazel-colored eyes. Y'all will make some pretty babies."

My heart panged at the mention of babies, but I shook Loryn and Tray out of my mind.

"You really think I should call him?"

"Yes. Especially since Loryn and Tray out here taking ultrasound pictures and shit."

"Oh, so you saw that?"

Becky sucked her teeth. "Loryn got some shit coming her way, I swear. God don't like ugly."

"Agreed, but ain't nothing nobody can do while she's pregnant."

Becky was silent for a moment. "Right," she said finally.

"Ugh, I don't want to call this man and then he be on some bullshit."

"You'll never know until you try. Go ahead and do it."

"Becky, I'm scared."

"We can do three-way."

"Nosey ass!"

"Shit, I'm just trying to help."

"Ugh, fine. I'll call him."

"Do it now, then call me back when you finish... unless y'all end up *talking all night.*"

She said the last part of her sentence in a deep baritone type voice.

I giggled. "Girl, shut up. Let me get off this phone and call him before I chicken out again."

Becky hung up on me.

I rolled my eyes and went to Noland's name in my contacts.

69

Tray

This shit was crazy.

I couldn't believe I lost my girl and got another bitch pregnant, just that quick.

Loryn needed to stop with that stupid shit, too. I went to the ultrasound appointment with her because I was stepping up to the plate as a man.

Then her stupid ass caught me off guard and took a picture of us like we were a couple.

When she did that, my mind went straight to Mia.

"Yo, delete that shit."

"Why?" Loryn whined.

"Because you being messy. You told Mia that me and you were in a relationship and you know that's a bold-faced lie."

She rolled her eyes. "Tray, not everything I do is for messy purposes. I'm taking pictures to document the journey for a scrapbook for our baby."

When she said that, I felt like an asshole.

My mind was so heavy on Mia, I zoned out on the fact that I really had a child on the way. That revelation hit me like a ton of bricks.

I was really about to be a father, and I was nowhere near ready.

I always told myself If I ever had a kid, I wanted to do it the right way.

I always saw Mia as the future mother of my babies, not Loryn.

This shit was fucked up beyond belief.

"Tray," Loryn said, her voice soft.

"What?"

"What do you think about us trying it out? For the baby?"

She looked down at her stomach, then up at me with tears in her eyes.

For the first time since this bullshit started, I sensed a sincerity in her.

"Loryn... I honestly can't think about this right now. My mind is on finding a way to get Mia back."

"Still?" She raised her eyebrows.

"What you mean, still?" I countered.

"Tray, if she hasn't answered your phone calls in over a month, it's time for you to let it go."

"She's just mad right now."

"How long are you going to wait on her?"

I was getting pissed off. "Look, that's really none of your concern. I would appreciate it if you kept all conversations between me and you about the kid."

"The kid, huh?" She looked hurt. "You are talking about my child as if he or she is a thing and not a person."

"We don't know what it is yet."

"Whatever, Tray."

Again, I felt bad for being offensive, but at the same time, fuck Loryn. It was her fault we were in this predicament in the first place.

No, it's your fault, too, my conscience reminded me.

I thought back to that night at the club.

If I could turn back the hands of time, I would have never even gone out.

Who knew a silly argument would lead to all this? I didn't even remember what me and Mia were fighting about.

While my mind was on Mia, the nurse called us. Loryn and I went through the appointment, and I couldn't front, I got a little teary eyed when I heard the baby's heartbeat. I low key wanted it to be a boy, and even envisioned myself playing catch with my future son.

Then I snapped out of it and resumed feeling like a piece of shit.

This wasn't right.

It was supposed to be Mia on that hospital bed, not Loryn.

When I got home, I was disgusted to see that Loryn had posted the picture of me and her and the sonogram photo, and tagged Mia.

See, this was that shit I was talking about.

Loryn was so full of shit, I wasn't sure which way was up.

At that moment, my phone buzzed with a text message from a random number.

You need a DNA test, asap.

I frowned. What the hell?

I texted back. *Who is this?*

Don't worry about who I am. Just get the test.

I called the number, but it kept ringing, then went to voicemail.

I tried again, but whoever it was blocked me.

"What the fuck is going on here?"

Chapter 10: Mia

Noland and I started dating... and he was perfect.

He was a complete gentleman, opening doors, listening when I talked, and even encouraging me when I cried about Tray.

I didn't know what to do because I liked Noland... but he wasn't Tray.

I still felt like me and Tray were incomplete.

I really thought we would be together forever.

Was this how every breakup felt? My mind swung so far from pole to pole that I felt like I was going crazy. One moment, I was desperately in love with Tray and wanted to call him and tell him to come back home. The other, I hated him with a passion and wanted to stab him right in his heart. Where he hurt me.

Yeah, I was probably crazy.

Good afternoon, Beautiful.

I dropped my fork when I saw the notification and smiled. I was sitting in my kitchen eating one of those frozen chicken alfredo dinners and drinking some apple juice. I felt like a little ass kid warming up frozen dinners rather than cooking, but my mind was still in and out of a depression.

Noland sent me afternoon texts every day. He worked third shift at a factory, so he was usually asleep throughout the morning.

Hey handsome, I texted back.

Can I take you out this weekend?

I stared at his text as I thought about it. We had been going on dates for the past three weekends, but regardless of how much distance there was between me and Tray's relationship, I felt like I was on two different time clocks. My time away from Tray and my time moving toward Noland.

For me and Tray, it had been seventy-six days since we last talked.

For me and Noland, we'd been dating for a month.

I couldn't deal.

As my mind was consumed with men, Evelin walked past me with a limp. She had one crutch that she was using to help her. All of our coworkers had fawned all over her when she came back to work. She didn't tell them I pushed her, but she made it a point to look in my direction whenever she talked about the "incident".

She always seemed to make her way into the coffee room while I was in there, and while she was there, she would put on a show like she was in deep pain so everyone could ask about her fall. I wanted to punch her in the face.

I curled my lip up at her in disgust as she eased into her seat in an exaggeratedly slow fashion, still not believing she had made up that bullshit story to Jessica about me pushing her. I felt bad that her fall had caused her to break her ankle, but I wasn't the one who pushed her and she knew it. For all I knew, she was being clumsy and fell, but I knew I couldn't say anything to her since I was on thin ice with my supervisor as it was.

I took my mind off her and did some work.

After a couple of hours of wrestling in my mind about whether I should go out with Noland, I went to Becky's name in my contacts to shoot her a text, making sure I checked that neither Evelin nor Jessica was watching since people were putting out complaints and shit. I typed out a message asking for advice, then paused. Becky would tell me to just snap out of it, to let Tray go, and to move forward with Noland, but I couldn't help it.

I wanted my man back.

I erased my message and put my phone away.

***

I headed to The Cafeteria myself to get some Italian food this time. I decided to give the tacos a break. I ran into Jeff.

He showed up three days a week to eat lunch.

Sometimes his dog was with him, and other times, he came with just his stick.

I greeted him as I sat down at his table.

"Hi, Mia, you over that jerk yet?"

I shook my head, forgetting he couldn't see the gesture. I hadn't told Jeff about Noland, but as I thought about it, I wondered if he could give me advice from a man's perspective.

"No, I'm not, but I have a problem."

Jeff perked up. "Oh?"

I blew out a breath. "Jeff, I know we don't know each other very well, but I'm wondering if I could ask you about something?"

"What is it, baby girl? You know I got your back."

He repositioned himself in his seat, then crossed his legs and clasped his hands over his knee. I studied his fresh buzz cut and business casual attire and suddenly wondered what Jeff did for a living.

Duh, he's on disability! my mind told me. Then I wondered if he was born blind, or had had an accident or something. He did give me a card with his name and phone number the day Tray had come to The Cafeteria. His name and number were literally all that was written on the card, but still... *Don't ask that,* I told myself, and focused back on the matter at hand.

I told him about me and Tray's breakup and him having a baby with Loryn. Then I told him about how I met Noland and had been seeing him for the past month. "Now I don't know what to do," I finished. "Do I go back or move forward?"

Jeff sighed. "First of all, let's clear the elephant out of the room."

My forehead creased, then he continued.

"You clearly didn't give me a chance, so I guess I'm not your type." He cleared his throat. "I suppose I can accept that, though since I've been seeing someone myself."

My jaw dropped.

"Who you been seeing?"

I had no idea why I felt a little jealous. Maybe it was because Jeff had been showing me so much love since we first met.

Jeff smirked. "That's neither here nor there, but just to let you know, she's a very nice lady, but back to your situation. For some reason, I don't like this Noland character."

My eyebrows raised. "You don't like Noland? Why?"

Jeff shrugged. "Just a hunch. Tray seems like the better bet, despite his infractions. You might want to have a full conversation with him since you haven't done that yet. What are you so afraid of?"

His question came so abruptly, it caught me off guard.

"What do you mean, what am I afraid of?"

"You said it's been over two months, and you haven't given the guy a conversation, yet you were in a relationship with him for five years. Did you really love him? Are you afraid he didn't really love you? What's up with that?"

I immediately felt defensive. "He cheated on me!"

Jeff paused. "Yet you can't get your mind off of him."

"We were together for five years."

"Indeed, you were."

I waited for Jeff to continue, but he didn't. Instead, he finished his turkey and cheese sandwich and got up to leave.

"See you later, Mia. I trust you'll make the right decision in the end."

I had no idea what to think of that conversation.

When I got back to my desk, I saw a bouquet of red roses sitting there.

"What in the world?" I wrinkled my nose.

Evelin turned in her seat. "Hmph," she said, then turned back around.

I shot her a weird look behind her back. Bitch.

I picked the card out of the bouquet, hoping it was from Tray.

It wasn't.

Beautiful roses for a beautiful lady.

-Noland

It was so simple, yet so sweet.

I had never been so torn in my life.

***

I decided to take Noland up on his date offer for this weekend. It wasn't like we hadn't been going on dates every weekend up to this point anyway.

He took me to a paint and sip. I had never been to one before, but as soon as we walked in, I fell in love with the atmosphere.

The lighting was soft, and the event was clearly set up for couples because the easels were placed two by two throughout the room, but they were all facing a podium in the front, which was situated on a small stage that had one step leading up to it.

The podium was standing next to a microphone, where I presumed the host would be giving us instructions.

Noland and I grabbed a courtesy bottle of Red Zinfandel.

"Oh wow, we might have to take it easy with this one," I said. I knew Zinfandel had a higher alcohol content than most wines.

Noland shrugged. "We'll be fine. It's just wine." They also had assortments of cheeses and crackers they were giving out. I grabbed one of those and brought it to the small table that separated me and Noland's easels.

The event coordinator walked up to the microphone.

"Good evening, Everyone."

Everyone stopped their chatter to give the man, Jared, their attention.

"We are going to do things a little differently tonight. The theme for the evening is *Art Therapy, Wine, and Relaxation*. We will be hosted by world-renowned poet and motivational speaker, The Mathematician. This man doesn't need much of an introduction, so I'll just let him take the floor."

There was light applause as the event coordinator left the stage and The Mathematician stepped up to the microphone and placed a black three-ring binder on the podium. He also was dressed in all black, complete with black shades and a black beret cocked to the side on his head.

He cleared his throat before speaking, and when he opened his mouth, I knew all the ladies in the room had the exact same response. *This nigga can get it!*

His voice was a combination of the syrupy sweetness of R&B artist, Neyo, and somehow, some way, Barry White.

It was unreal.

I glanced at Noland and I could tell he was slightly intimidated by the way The Mathematician was captivating the female audience.

"Peace and Love to you all," The Mathematician said. "As Jared said, tonight we are going to do something a little different. I'm going to take you through a range of emotions. At some points, the feeling might get a little intense, but just keep up with me, and we'll make it through together. Is that alright?"

The way The Mathematician set up the event was to perform six of his pieces that were going to bring us through what he called Seasons of Change, based on the stages of grief after going through a significant loss in life.

I wasn't sure I was ready for something like this.

I looked at Noland, but he was focused on his easel.

I wondered if he knew tonight was going to be structured like a therapy session?

I didn't know how to feel about that.

Since we were here, however, I decided to just go through with it. Maybe it would help with my emotions.

The Mathematician went through each of his pieces in the order of the stages of grief. Denial, Anger, Bargaining, Depression, Acceptance, and Hope.

With each poem, he combined a bit of singing, rap, and poetry to get you all the way into whatever emotion the poem was representing.

Our instructions were to paint whatever came to our mind at the time, and to take a little wine when needed.

Needless to say, by the time the event was over, me and Noland's bottle was demolished, with me drinking the majority of it.

I was so into The Mathematician's words and my easel that I barely even noticed Noland still in the room with me.

"Damn, that was intense!" I said.

I flipped through the pages of paintings I had made. I did six different ones. One for each poem. Each one brought something different out of me. I didn't know what to feel, but I wanted to frame these and put them in my living room or something.

"Damn, those are good," Noland mused.

I didn't think my paintings were all that great. They were more like splashes of color, but anyone could definitely tell which emotion I was feeling based on the colors of the paintings. My anger and depression paintings were my favorites.

As one could imagine, the anger one was various shades of red with angry looking lines and aggressive and jagged images. My depression one was shades of blue, and the lines were loopier and more directionless.

"Damn, I need some more art therapy in my life!" I chuckled. I turned to Noland's easel. "Let's see what you came up with."

Noland looked nervous all of a sudden.

"Well, mine isn't as magnificent as yours."

I blushed. "Magnificent?"

Noland didn't respond. He just cleared his throat.

"Well, I didn't do six different paintings like you. I just did one."

"That's fine," I reassured him. "The Mathematician said it didn't matter how many paintings you did, as long as you painted how you feel."

Noland went to his easel and flipped back the page that was covering his painting.

My jaw dropped, and suddenly I felt heat running through me.

I was staring at a perfect portrait of myself, down to the blue butterfly clip I was wearing in my hair.

"Noland, this is beautiful!" I said, in awe of him. I couldn't stop staring at the portrait. Noland had me mesmerized.

***

I woke up the next morning to soft music playing downstairs in the kitchen.

"Tray?" I whispered, then my memories came back to me.

I was naked and a little sore down there.

I blushed as I remembered how Noland made love to me the night before. It was everything I had expected, and more. He knew how to be soft and gentle, yet firm and aggressive when necessarily.

I snapped out of it.

"Oh my God, I can't believe I did that!"

I wasn't sure I was completely ready to cross that threshold with Noland like that. He was cool and charming and everything, but my heart was still with Tray.

"Shit!"

I grabbed my robe and slipped my feet into my slippers to make my way down the stairs.

I smelled pancakes and burnt sausage as I crossed the living room to enter the kitchen.

Noland was standing over the stove, humming along with the song that was playing on his phone.

He turned and saw me. "Hey!" His eyes lit up.

I didn't know what to say. He looked so happy to see me. I was happy to see him too, especially after the night we shared, but at the same time I wanted him to leave. I couldn't just kick him out though. "Hey," I said instead, and sat down.

Noland turned the stove off and fixed our plates.

"I hope you don't mind, but I like a little black on my sausages," he remarked. His sausages were almost completely black, while mine had a little bit of black, but mostly a regular tone.

"Thank you."

We started eating, and although it was a peaceful breakfast, I still felt awkward as hell.

Noland made small talk, and I responded in all the right places, but I couldn't bring myself to say what I really wanted to say.

When we finished, I finally felt a sense of relief.

"Well, Mia, I gotta head out. I told my boss I would come in and do a few hours today."

"Oh, that's fine! We'll talk later."

He moved to kiss me before he left, and I kissed him, but it didn't feel good. I felt like a traitor.

This whole situation was confusing me. I wanted Noland, but I didn't want him. I wanted Tray, but I didn't want him either.

When Noland left, I burst into tears.

Chapter 11: Mia

Just as I finished washing the last dish and putting it in my dishrack, Becky knocked on my front door, popping up on me.

"Well, hello to you!" she said. "How was your date last night?"

"The date was fine."

She gave me a knowing look. "And...?"

"And what?" I felt hella uneasy all of a sudden.

Becky stared at me expectantly for a second, then she lost her patience. "Bitch, how was it? I drove past earlier because I was gonna stop by, but I saw an extra car in the driveway." She gave me a knowing look after that.

"Becky, I feel horrible."

"Horrible? Why?"

"Because I had sex with Noland."

"And?"

I opened my mouth to respond, but we heard a knock on the door.

"Who is that?" Becky asked. "I know he ain't coming back for more."

She went over and opened the door.

It was Tray.

"Mia..." he said, but his voice trailed off when he saw that it was Becky who answered his knocking.

"What are you doing here?" Becky asked, shooting him an accusatory glare.

"I came to talk to my woman."

"She's no longer yours. She found someone new. You should too."

Both me and Tray had the same expression on our faces after that, but for different reasons.

"Becky, what the fuck is wrong with you?" I screeched, at the same time that Tray said, "Found another nigga?!"

"I'll leave now," Becky said, and she exited my apartment.

Tray turned on me. "What she mean, you found another nigga, Mia?"

"It's been three months, Tray. Ain't you with Loryn now?"

"You know good and goddamn well I ain't with Loryn if I been blowing up your phone."

"Didn't stop you from blowing up hers when we were together."

"Who is this other nigga?"

"Does it matter?" My eyes narrowed.

"Did you fuck him?"

Tray's question came so fast, I didn't have time to process it.

There was no need. He read my facial expression. "You did?"

My heart dropped as I saw the look on his face.

"Last night."

He was wounded by my words, I could tell.

One part of me didn't give a damn, and said it served him right, but another part of me was heartbroken right along with him.

"Mia... Mia, how did we get here?"

"I don't know, Tray," I answered truthfully.

"I don't know, either."

He stepped toward me, and I didn't move away.

"I miss you."

My lower lip trembled. "I miss you, too."

85

"I need you."

I didn't respond to that, but Tray stepped up on me and I became lost in his scent. I missed it so much. He was wearing one of the Versace colognes I had bought him for his birthday.

I needed him, too, in the worst way.

What me and Tray had was deeper than anything I ever had with another man.

Next thing I knew, we were kissing, but then I snapped out of it.

"We can't," I said.

"Mia, I don't give a fuck what you did with that nigga. I need you right now."

His gaze was so intense that when he started kissing me again, I didn't stop him.

It felt so right, yet so wrong at the same time as I let Tray take control of me, as he had done so many times before.

Before I knew it, my robe was off and Tray was stepping out of his shorts.

I couldn't help it. I didn't want to.

We made love right there on the hardwood floor.

It was magical, but when it was over, my back was hurting like a motherfucker.

"Ugh, get off of me," I said, and Tray rolled over.

I blinked, then I felt like the nastiest bitch ever.

I was clearly mentally unstable, seeing that I just made the two worst mistakes of my life, back-to-back.

"Get out," I said to Tray, just as he was opening his mouth to say something to me.

"What?" He looked surprised.

"I said get out, Tray." I stood and put my robe on, trying to cover up the shameful feeling that was rising within me.

"Mia, we just…"

"I don't care what we just did. You took advantage of me. You both did."

"What?"

Tray stood as well.

I shook my head. "Just get the hell out. Now."

He stared at me for a few more moments, then he put his clothes back on and left.

***

Becky looked like she wanted to burst through the phone and strangle me after I finished telling her what happened.

We were on FaceTime. I was so distraught after Tray left that I didn't know what to do, so I called her.

"You mean to tell me that you fucked Noland, then kicked me out to fuck Tray? Girl, what the hell is wrong with you?"

"Becky, it all just happened so fast."

"No, Mia. Unh uh. You gonna have to reign this shit in, girl because you're getting out of control. I never should have left you alone with him. I should have stood my ground and kicked his ass out."

She was pissing me off with her blunt tone. "Who the fuck are you? My mother?"

"Excuse me? I'm over here trying to be your friend."

I calmed. "Becky, look I know what I did was wrong, but my mind is all over the place."

"Clearly."

Becky's tone was harsh, but I knew it was only out of concern for me.

Something had to give.

Chapter 12: Mia

It had been a week and both Noland and Tray had been blowing up my phone.

I felt disgusting for having sex with them both back-to-back like that, but Becky was right. I need to get my emotions in check.

I rolled my eyes as yet another text came through on my phone from Noland, followed by one from Tray.

What, did they sense each other trying to contact me or something?

Granted, Noland didn't know I slept with Tray directly after sleeping with him, but...

"Ugh!" I plopped my head in my hands.

I needed to take control of this situation.

I sent a group text to Noland and Tray, so I only had to do this once. I set the replies to only come to me, however, since I didn't want them beefing with each other as a result of my actions.

Listen,

My mind is not right at this time. I'm going through too much and I would appreciate it if you left me alone and gave me a chance to process this situation. This is the only time I'm going to ask.

Contact me again, and you're blocked.

Of course, neither one of them listened to what I said. Both of them texted me again immediately. This time it was Tray first, then Noland. I had no idea why I unblocked Tray from my phone in the first place.

Well, I kind of did, since we...

"That's it! I'm done!"

Tray's picture flashed in my phone as he tried to call me.

I rejected the call, then blocked both he and Noland's numbers.

***

And, of course, I was pregnant.

Fuck my life.

I found out two weeks later. I was just starting to get to the point where I was unsorting the confusion I faced by starting something with Noland when I wasn't fully over Tray.

I also forgave myself for sleeping with them back-to-back. My mind wasn't functioning properly. I just took it as an L and decided to keep moving.

Then my period didn't come, which I noticed because it came every twenty-eight days without fail.

I looked up some articles online and found that sometimes stress could cause a period to fluctuate, but I wasn't taking any chances.

I got a couple tests from the dollar store and they all came back positive.

Now I had no idea what the hell I was about to do.

Tray

Loryn texted me asking me to come by her house today after work so we could talk about the baby.

I decided to go since this seemed like my fate now.

I couldn't believe I was in this situation, yo. Five years with the love of my life down the drain over some bullshit. I wanted to find that nigga Mia was messing with.

I knew if I did, however, it would only lead to more trouble.

I just wanted my baby back.

A text came through on my phone. *Did you get it yet?*

It was that same random number from before. I guess they unblocked me.

Who is this? I texted back.

That doesn't matter. Did you get the test?

Why the hell was this person so concerned? It was obviously somebody that knew me, but why wouldn't they just come out and say who they were?

"You good, bro?" I turned to see Trevor staring at me. I was in the middle of stocking some laundry soaps, while he was pretending to help me to get a break from being outside all day.

"Nah, man. I keep getting text messages from this random number, but they don't want to tell me who they are."

His eyebrows raised. "Random messages saying what?"

"Telling me to get a DNA test."

Just then, Ricardo, my supervisor walked by. "Hey! Tray, we don't pay you to stand here and mingle. The laundry soaps should have been restocked twenty minutes ago."

I was gonna say something back, but decided against it. I already had enough drama in my life. I didn't need even more from Ricardo.

Ricardo turned to Trevor. "What are you doing in this section? Don't you work outside with the carts?"

Trevor went back outside, and I resumed stocking.

I went through the rest of my shift without incident, then headed to Loryn's house.

When I pulled up, there was an extra car in her driveway.

A nigga came out of her apartment, gave me a funny look, then got in his car and drove off.

When I knocked on the door, Loryn looked surprised to see me.

"Who was that?" I asked.

"What are you doing here?" she asked.

"You asked me to come by after work." My eyes narrowed.

She gave me a strange look. "No, I didn't."

I pulled out my phone. I didn't have time for this shit. "Here," I said, extending it to her.

She looked embarrassed. "I don't remember sending that."

"Anyway, it must not have been nothing important. Who was the nigga that just left?"

Her eyes shifted. "Nobody."

"Loryn..."

"What, Tray?" She crossed her arms over her chest.

"Stop playing with me."

91

"I'm not playing with you. I told you he was nobody, so you need to just believe me. Besides, you said you don't want a relationship with me, anyway. Why are you so concerned?"

"Because if you fucking another nigga then we need a DNA test. That's why."

She got mad. "How dare you call me a fucking hoe!"

"Nobody said you was a hoe."

"You might as well, asking for a DNA test like I just go give my shit to anybody."

I almost opened my mouth to say she fucked me knowing I was drunk and in a serious relationship with her best friend, but I decided against it. I didn't need this headache today.

"Look, Loryn. I didn't come over here to argue with you. I'm not calling you a hoe, but I still want a test."

"Fuck you, Tray."

She slammed the door in my face.

***

The next morning, I woke up to see that Loryn texted me, apologizing.

Sorry for yelling yesterday, Tray. I didn't mean to lash out. I just been stressed.

I texted her back to say we were good.

I wasn't good, though. I called out of work. I needed a day to clear my mind.

Chapter 13: Mia

I figured I couldn't keep Noland and Tray in the dark since I was pregnant with one of their babies. Not only had I slept with them back-to-back, I didn't use protection with either of them. Tray and I never used protection, but with Noland, my inhibitions were lowered by all the alcohol I consumed. Plus, I was caught up in the moment after he drew that portrait of me. *No excuses, Mia,* my mind said. This was a big ass mess. I hadn't told anyone else the news yet. I knew Becky would probably blow a gasket.

If this baby was Tray's, I didn't know how I was gonna feel.

To find out he got my best friend pregnant, then got me pregnant right after?

This was crazy.

My finger hovered over Tray's name in my contacts to unblock him, then I chickened out and went to click on Noland's name instead.

I chickened out again and texted my mother.

Mommy... was all I said.

What is it? was her rapid reply.

I did a bad thing.

Seconds later, my phone rang. "Hello?" I answered.

"What kind of bad thing did you do, Mia?" My mother's voice was full of concern.

I decided to come right out with it. "Got pregnant."

She was silent for a moment, then sighed. "I guess congratulations are in order. Have you told Tray yet?"

I didn't respond.

"Mia?"

"It might not be his."

My mom tried to video call me, but I rejected it. "Unh uh, little girl. What do you mean it might not be Tray's?"

My eyes clouded. "I made a mistake."

"Who did you sleep with?"

"This guy I met. We haven't been dating long."

My mother fell silent again. "Damn, Mia," she finally said.

"I feel so ashamed." I felt like a little girl exposing myself to her like this.

"Honey, we all make mistakes. Heck, I've made quite a few over my life, but I think you should contact both of these men and tell them what's going on. Wait, there are only two, right?"

"Mom!" I said, the horror evident in my tone.

"I wasn't saying it like that, Mia. I just know how heartbreak can work sometimes."

The way she said that had me tearing up again. "No, it was only those two. I feel so disgusting."

"Like I said, we all make mistakes. At this point, the only thing you can do is put on your big girl panties and tell Tray and this mystery man what's going on. Who is the mystery man, anyway? Have I met him?"

"No, you haven't. His name is Noland."

"Noland, huh? What does he do, fix computers?"

I chuckled. "No. He works at a factory."

"Oh. Well, do you think he would be the type to step up to the plate if the child is his?"

I blew out a breath. "I hope so." During the course of this conversation with my mother, I felt my shame going away and empowerment rising to the surface. My mom always knew how to get me right.

94

"You know what you have to do now. Call me if you need anything."

We hung up, and I felt nervous all over again, but then I decided to just buckle down and do it.

My mind went to Noland first, but my fingers ended up at Tray's name. I unblocked him and called.

"Hello?" he answered on the second ring.

"Tray, I need to talk to you."

He was silent for a second. "Okay. Do you want me to stop by or you want to meet somewhere?"

My heart burned at the fact that he was so ready to see me after I blocked him for such a long time. He had given me my space as I asked him to, but I could tell from his tone of voice that he was nowhere near done with me, as I was nowhere near done with him. For life, in fact, if this baby was his.

I swallowed. Why did it have to be this way?

"You can stop by," I finally said.

Tray was at the door twenty minutes later. "Hey." He moved to hug me, then stopped himself.

I wanted to hug him, too, but I didn't make any motions.

We ambled over to the couch, and my mind was inundated with flashbacks. All the times we spent on this couch, and on the loveseat. Making love.

Then my eyes traveled to the hardwood floor where we made our baby.

If it was his...

"Mia?" Tray asked.

I snapped out of it. "Huh?"

"What did you want to talk about? Did you want to give us another chance?"

I took a deep breath. "Tray, I don't know how else to tell you this, so I'll just say it: I'm pregnant."

His eyes popped open a little wider when he heard the news. Then he looked elated. "Are you sure? How far along are you?"

My face fell, and he looked confused until I said my next words. "Six weeks."

He made an unintelligible sound, then said, "You're saying you don't know if it's me or him?"

I shook my head.

We stared at each other for a while.

"Mia, why don't we just put everything behind us and start over?"

I snorted. "We can't exactly do that so easily since you have a baby on the way with my ex-best friend!"

My tone was so sudden and snappy, it startled both of us.

"Mia, I swear it wasn't like that."

"Right, because you were drunk? Don't make excuses for your bullshit, Tray."

"I'm not making excuses. We had a fight that night. I was at the club with Anthony and Trevor. Becky and Loryn were there, and Anthony and Trevor ended up leaving me trying to get with some bitches. Loryn gave me a ride home."

"Hmph. A ride home wasn't all she gave you." Before I could block them, images flooded my mind of Loryn and Tray having sex.

Vomit rushed to my throat and I ran to the half-bath that was between the living room and kitchen to empty my insides into the toilet.

Tray followed behind me. "Is that morning sickness?" he asked, handing me a paper towel.

I snatched it. "Wouldn't you fucking know!"

I wet the paper towel then cleaned my face. I felt miserable. Was this what my life was going to be like?

Losing the love of my life in such a messed up way, then holding onto a piece of him through our child? As if he was hearing my thoughts, Tray said, "Mia, we can still work this out."

"How, when you have a whole baby with Loryn, Tray?"

Loryn. I hadn't said her name out loud in such a long time. My mind was still reeling over what she had done to me even though so much time had passed. I really thought that girl was my best friend, my rider. I certainly rode for her. More times than I could count.

"You know what?" I said, with an air of finality in my tone. "I can't do this, Tray. If the baby is yours, we will just have to work something out, but I can't be with you knowing you did what you did, and didn't even bother to tell me until a child came from it."

For the first time, Tray was left without words. What could he say? There was no comeback for what he did to me. To us.

I choked up again as I thought of how we were about to get married before all this happened. Maybe God had worked it out. He didn't let me have to deal with a lifetime of heartache and betrayal by a man I loved with all my heart, and who I thought loved me back. "I think you should go," I said, my voice barely above a whisper.

"Mia, I love you."

I couldn't look at him. I loved him too, but this was something I could not bear.

"Learn to love Loryn," was all I could muster while staring at the bathroom wall.

Tray stood there for a long time staring at me while I willed myself not to look back before he trudged toward the front door and walked out of my life.

I would be a goddamn liar if I said my heart didn't go with him. I broke down.

**

After my breakdown, I felt empty inside. I wanted to call Becky and tell her to bring some drinks, then I remembered I was pregnant. Plus, Becky didn't know about the baby yet and I wasn't trying to have her yelling in my ear.

I was lying on the hardwood floor. Call me crazy, but I collapsed there after Tray walked out and couldn't bring myself to get up.

The floor was warm underneath me. I knew by now the side of my face was probably red from being against it for so long.

A knock sounded at my door. I didn't want to answer it, but I knew I couldn't be childish for the rest of my life.

I slowly rose from the floor and went to see who it was. When I opened it, Noland stood before me.

"What are you doing here?" I asked.

He looked concerned. "Mia, what happened to your face?"

"Huh?" I touched it, then I remembered. I shook my head. "Nothing. Why are you here?"

He looked like he wanted to question me further about my face, but decided against it. "I needed to see you. I know you said you wanted space, but it's been a few weeks, Mia."

I sighed. *Might as well get this over with now.*

"Come in. I need to talk to you, anyway."

Noland entered my apartment and we went to sit on the couch, ironically, the same way Tray and I did earlier, except it wasn't the same.

Nothing would ever be the same. Not without Tray.

"What did you want to talk about?" Noland asked. He looked like he was excited. *Probably thinks I want to get back with him,* I reasoned. *Do I?*

Noland and I technically weren't official when we were together, but he never gave me any bad vibes. Still, I felt horrible after sleeping with him, though I did like him. I realized I was still confused, but If I was really moving on from Tray, why not give Noland a chance? He'd been nothing but sweet and understanding to me. Maybe God sent him to help me heal.

"Noland, I know this probably isn't something you're prepared to hear, but I'm pregnant."

His jaw dropped. "What?"

I nodded.

"You're serious?"

"Yes. I found out a couple of weeks ago."

Noland sat there processing what I just told him. "Wow, Mia. This is unexpected. What do you want to do?"

I got a little offended by the way he said that. "What do you mean, what do I want to do? What do you want to do?" I shot him an accusatory glare.

He held his hands up. "Wait, not like that. I meant I know in society it's considered your decision since it's your body, but I have to tell you I don't believe in abortions. Even if you don't want to be with me, I would love to have the child and raise him on my own."

Now it was my turn to do a jaw-drop. "You're okay with me being pregnant this soon?"

Then I remembered he didn't know about me sleeping with Tray.

Noland shrugged. "It happens. As a man, I should have known what was possible when we slept together. I've never been one to shy away from responsibility."

Damn, I was liking Noland more and more. If this was the type of time he was on, we just might work.

I was ready to block Tray from my heart and mind, if it was possible, but still, Noland needed to know the whole truth.

"Noland, there's just one problem."

"Your ex?" he asked, as if he already knew.

I blinked. "Yeah. How did you know?"

"I figured you weren't finished with him. I was trying to give you time while we were dating. Is there a possibility the baby is his?" While Noland was talking, he looked like he was more concerned for me and my feelings than he was for his own.

Damn, that's the kind of man I need. Tray's ass got my best friend pregnant and was ready to leave me in the dark about them even sleeping together.

I nodded, then studied his expression. He understood.

"It might be a challenge if the baby is his, but I know in my heart that he's mine."

I chuckled, happy that this situation was starting to work itself out. "How are you so sure? Do you have any other children?"

He shook his head. "I don't, but I've wanted one for years. I was just trying to find the right woman."

The look in his eyes when he said that was mesmerizing. I felt the heat rising within me.

"What do you say, Mia? Can we give our relationship another try?"

I didn't bother correcting him by telling him we were never official. "Sounds good to me," I said instead.

Tray

Me, Anthony, and Trevor sat around Ant's table playing Rummy. Trev was dealing while me and Ant were talking about my situation.

"I can't believe my whole relationship is down the drain."

Ant looked like he felt for me. "I know, man. I definitely thought you and Mia would end up married."

Trev passed out the last card, then picked up his hand. "I still think you should get that DNA test on Loryn, ASAP."

Me and Ant nodded. "Right," I said, "That's a given, but what if the baby really is mine? Then Mia will never take me back."

I didn't want to tell them that there was a possibility Mia's baby wasn't mine, either, but maybe I was deceiving myself. I had one kid and a possible. My life was like a game of spades.

"You just gotta deal with it as it comes, Tray," Ant said as he studied his cards.

"Right."

We played a few more games, then called it quits.

After we finished, Trev left to go with his girl and Ant went with his girl, so I was left at home. Sooner or later, Ant was probably gonna want me to move out, but I knew he hadn't said anything up to this point because he was trying to look out for me.

Loryn texted my phone. *Hey. You busy?*

No.

She called me.

"Hello?" I answered.

"Why you sound so depressed?" she asked.

I didn't respond.

"Anyway, I wanted to talk to you about something."

"What is it?" I thought she was about to ask for something related to the baby.

"What do you think about me and you giving our relationship a try?"

Not this BS again.

I snorted. "Me and you don't have a relationship, Loryn. In case you forgot, I was just engaged to your best friend."

"But you still slept with me, though."

"And according to your own words, I was drunk and thought I was with Mia." I thought at that moment how bogus that sounded, but I did wake up in her bed.

"Listen, I didn't call you to start a fight. I'm just trying to think this through as an adult. Are you not attracted to me or something? If we have a child together we might as well make it work. I don't want my baby growing up in a single parent home."

"Mia's pregnant, too," I blurted out before I could stop myself.

"What?" Loryn's reply came out in a strangled tone. "You're still sleeping with her?"

"If I was?" I looked at my phone like, *what the fuck?*

"Tray, I thought y'all were broken up." Loryn sounded like she was hurt over my revelation.

"Why are you so bothered?"

"Because I'm about to have a child, and it looks like he or she will be neglected by their father."

Now I felt like a bastard again. "Loryn, no. I'm not about to diss the baby. If it is mine, I'm gonna step up to the plate. I'm not that type of nigga, Ma."

"But how are you gonna take care of two kids, though? How far along is Mia?"

"We just found out," I said, though I knew I was only playing myself. Mia ain't want shit to do with me. My bond with her was only in my fantasies.

"Wow, Tray." Loryn sniffled.

"Look, it's okay. We'll find a way to get through this. I don't know how I'm gonna take care of two kids, either, but I promise to be in both of their lives."

"Yeah," she said, then hung up.

I wondered if I went too far by telling Loryn that Mia was pregnant. It was clear she and Mia didn't fuck with each other anymore, so it really wasn't Loryn's business...

This shit was too much for me.

I went to the cabinet and grabbed Ant's last bottle of Henny. I'd have to pay him back later.

Chapter 14: Mia

I was starting to show. This pregnancy was scary as hell for me because I never expected it to happen, but Noland had been the perfect gentleman every step of the way.

Tray called me on the regular, too, but I told him Noland and I were in a relationship. I think I broke his heart, but he broke mine first, so whatever.

I couldn't shake him from my mind, though, despite the fact that I'd moved on.

Every time I thought of Tray, however, I thought of Loryn and the fact that she was probably around six or seven months by now. Pretty soon, Tray would have a lot to handle.

I wondered for a while if Tray took me up on my suggestion and got with Loryn, but judging from the fact that her relationship status on social media hadn't changed and there were no new photos posted, except for her baby bump, I guessed he didn't.

Plus, he still tried to inbox and text me about us getting back together.

I mostly ignored him, but sometimes I considered blocking him out of respect for Noland.

At the same time, I couldn't fully block him because he might have actually been the father.

"Ugh! I can't wait til this baby is out so I can get a DNA test."

I was feeling ashamed again. I knew my mom said we all made mistakes, but it was one thing to know that, and another to live it.

I felt like a Maury episode.

Things at work were slightly better now that Jessica had left the company and Evelin was now promoted to supervisor. I guess I should have put two and two together about Evelin vying for Jessica's position, because right before she started acting funny, Evelin mentioned to me that she was thinking of applying for a promotion.

"Would you ever want to be a supervisor?" she had asked.

I smirked at her and said, "Maybe."

I guess she took me seriously because apparently she must have found out Jessica was planning on leaving the company. Everyone knew I would be next in line since I had the most seniority on our team.

When I was in the coffee room one day after Evelin was promoted, I heard one of our coworkers scoffing about how Evelin had been kissing up to all the managers and supervisors for months, trying to put herself in the position to be chosen as supervisor.

She must have thought she needed to eliminate me to ensure her spot.

What Evelin did to get ahead of the game was fucked up, but I didn't have time to think about her. As long as she no longer fucked with me, I was over it.

I was back to openly texting on my phone during shifts since Jessica was gone and Evelin no longer even looked my way as she strode back and forth to her new office each day.

My phone buzzed with a text from Becky as I was finishing one of my claims. Becky had cursed me clean out when I first told her I was pregnant.

I knew she would be pissed, but I couldn't be fully mad at her, because she had been my rock through this whole situation with Tray and Noland.

Becky and I were going out today after we got off work to purchase maternity clothes. I pulled up to the store around the same time she did. We greeted each other with a hug, then entered the store.

"Are you and Noland thinking of moving in together?" she asked as we walked through the aisles, looking at the various selections.

I sighed. "He just suggested that the other day, but I don't think I'm ready."

Becky studied me. "Why not? Don't tell me you still stuck on Tray. Noland is a good man, Mia."

"I know he's a good man, but..."

"Hey!" we were interrupted by some female I didn't know. She walked up and hugged Becky, then looked at me.

"Mia, this is Tina," Becky said. "She's one of my clients."

"Hey Tina," I said.

Tina turned to Becky. "Girl, when is your salon opening again? You know Monica has been talking hella shit since you left, right?"

Becky had left Heavenly Tresses two weeks ago after a huge falling out with Monica. Apparently, one of her regulars missed his appointment time and came while she was doing someone else's hair, and Becky had done them both simultaneously instead of making him reschedule.

Monica took it as Becky being disrespectful, especially since Becky had voiced the fact that she disagreed with the new policy.

Becky lost her temper and cussed Monica out, telling her the only reason she was making the policy in the first place was because Bria tried to copy her and failed. Monica tried to fire Becky, but Becky said she quit.

Now Becky was looking into opening her own location with the money she had saved.

"Girl, I can't wait, either. Monica can say whatever she wants to say about me, but nobody can deny my skills."

Tina nodded. It was true. Becky had more clients than anyone at that salon, including Monica.

After Tina left, Becky and I picked out a few dresses and comfortable shoes. I heard sometimes a woman's feet would go up in size when she got pregnant, along with swelling. I hoped not because I had tons of cute shoes I didn't want to part with.

I felt my phone vibrate in my back pocket and saw that Noland texted me his customary message. *Good afternoon, Beautiful.*

I couldn't help but smile. If Noland was anything, he was consistent.

"Who's that? Ya man?" Becky said with a knowing smile of her own.

"Yup!" I texted him back and let myself be excited for once. I was pregnant and in a relationship with a man that cared about me. So what if it didn't work out in the way that I envisioned?

Tray

My internship offered me a job.

My first thought was to call Mia, but my excitement wouldn't be complete without her. She had stood strong in her decision for us to break up. She told me that the only reason we should ever talk again was if it was about the baby.

I couldn't help but to still want to call her though. This was what we wanted. For me to leave Walmart and get a job as a dental hygienist. Everything I worked hard for was going up in flames.

I blocked out those thoughts and texted Mia instead of calling. *My internship gave me a job.*

She didn't write back.

That hurt, but I guess I earned it. This was where we were now. I would have to face the fact that I lost my girl. The thing was, I used to be the player type right along with Trev and Ant, but when I met Mia, all the bullshit stopped.

Then, with the one woman I was faithful to, I fucked around on her and got caught up in the worst way.

That must have been that karma shit they be talking about.

I was really trying to do the right thing with her, though.

Just as I was pulling down the street toward Ant's house, the radio started playing throwbacks. Case's *Missing You* came on. I changed that shit real quick to another station. No luck there, either because that station was playing Neyo's *So Sick*. This was really some bullshit. I turned the radio off.

Loryn called me on my Bluetooth. A nigga couldn't catch a break these days.

"Hello?" I answered, trying my best to take the aggravation out of my tone.

"Tray," Loryn said in this whiny voice she recently developed since the baby was due any day now and I had become her slave.

"What is it?"

"Can you come over and give me another massage? My back is killing me."

I had been giving Loryn back massages and foot massages for the past few weeks. At first, I told her to go to a parlor for that shit, but then my mom got on me about doing my potential baby momma wrong.

"Tray, that girl didn't lay down to make that baby by herself. You laid down with her. Get over there and massage her back and her feet. She's carrying your child."

Whenever my mom talked in that stern tone, I knew I fucked up. I stopped acting like a boy and went over there. It was clear Loryn was not lying when she said she was tired and sore from her demeanor and facial expressions when I would go over her house.

Try as I might, though, I just couldn't get with it. I didn't know if I just wasn't cut out to be a father, or if it was the fact that I wished I was doing all this for Mia.

Mia wouldn't have even had to ask me. I guess I was being selfish.

I couldn't imagine that other nigga touching her...

"Tray, did you hear me?" Loryn's voice interrupted my thoughts.

"Yeah, I'm on my way," I said.

I did a three-point turn and started toward her house.

"Don't forget the fudge, please."

"Huh?" I blinked.

Loryn sounded impatient. "I asked you to get me some chocolate ice cream, Tray."

My ears burned with embarrassment. "Oh, my bad. I'm stopping at the store now."

"And chocolate fudge please."

"I gotchu." I hung up with Loryn and pulled into a convenience store parking lot to pick up the ice cream and fudge. Of course, they had one, but not the other, so I had to go to another store near Loryn's house to complete her request.

When I got to her house, I realized I had forgotten to pick up the massage oil she texted me and said she wanted when I was at the first store.

Oh well, she would just have to accept the ice cream.

I started to feel a little guilty as I went up her front steps. I needed to stop being an asshole and just accept my wrongs.

I knocked on her door, prepared to apologize for forgetting the oil, but Loryn called from the inside. "Come in! It's open."

Lazy ass didn't even want to get up to open the door, I thought, but then I felt like an asshole again. I really needed to work on that.

I exhaled, then opened the door.

I immediately became pissed again.

Loryn rose from her seat trying to look seductive. She was fully made up with her hair and nails done, and sporting a purple teddy that might as well have been nonexistent.

She walked toward me, and part of me couldn't front that she was sexy. Her nails and feet were painted purple, and her bare toes were turning me on a little.

I hadn't had none in a minute.

"This is what you called me for?" I asked, trying to keep my composure, but the closer she walked to me, the more that look in her eyes had me twisted. Conflicted.

Was I really about to fuck Loryn?

She smiled, probably noticing I was responding to her game. She played with her hair. "Why don't you close the door?"

I obeyed, and her smile widened.

"I forgot the oil," I said, still trying to hold back from making the second worst decision of my life.

She chuckled. "That's fine."

Now she was up on me, and she was smelling so good I almost lost it. Women were the devil, I swore. She rubbed her breasts against my chest, then her eyes flicked down toward my belt, then up to my eyes.

"Maybe I can help you relax before you help me."

I tried one more time. "Loryn, I really don't think we should be doing this."

I created a little distance between us by stepping back and holding up the bag of ice cream and fudge as a barrier. "I wasn't expecting nothing like this to go down. Ain't you about to have the baby, anyway?"

We both knew I was just grasping for straws because my words were saying one thing, but my body was saying another.

Loryn reached out and grabbed my mans through my pants.

"Come on, Tray. Hasn't it been a while? It has for me. You were the last man I slept with."

That made me snap out of it.

I recoiled so hard I could tell it hurt her feelings.

"What's wrong?"

"Fucking with you is why we in this predicament in the first place." I had finally snapped out of it, thank God. I walked over and put the bag of ice cream and fudge on her coffee table. "If you want your massage, we can do that, but I'm not doing anything else."

Loryn sucked her teeth.

"What the hell, Tray? You need to get over Mia. She's moved on, anyway. You should too."

"What are you talking about?" I felt the heat rising within me. I hadn't told Loryn about Mia's new boyfriend.

"Her relationship status changed," Loryn spat. "She got herself a new man, so you need to move on with me."

Loryn took a step forward, but fluid ran down her legs.

"Oh, shit," I said. "Are you peeing yourself?"

She looked mortified. "No."

It dawned on me what was really happening.

"We gotta go to the hospital. Where's your coat?"

Loryn got frantic. "I can't go looking like this, Tray! Help me get dressed."

We went to action and I helped her get out of the teddy and into something more decent. We drove in silence to the hospital, but by the time we got there, her contractions were starting.

Four hours later, a healthy baby girl was born.

Chapter 15: Mia

I couldn't help but stalk Loryn's page from time to time to see if there were any updates about Tray. I hadn't done it in over a week, but today, I didn't need to.

A picture came across my timeline with the caption, *She's here!*

Then I saw another one with Loryn holding her daughter, and another with Tray holding her. I couldn't take it.

I blocked Loryn. I had no idea why I didn't do that a long time ago.

Apparently, she and Tray had their baby yesterday.

I moped around at work and then at home, depressed over the fact that this was my new reality. Me and Tray were through. I still couldn't believe it.

I rubbed my belly as I felt my baby kick. I wondered if I was going to have a girl or boy? We hadn't had the test yet to figure out the baby's gender. Noland was so sure it was a boy, and he wanted him to be a junior.

I told him I didn't mind, if the child was his.

I had no idea what we were going to name her if it was a girl.

When I got home from work, I saw a large gift bag sitting on my front stoop. I rolled my eyes, but smiled at the same time. "Noland."

I approached the bag in nervous anticipation, then I bent at the waist to pick it up. When I straightened, I felt a wave of pain rush through my belly.

"Oh Lord, remind me to never do that again." I stood there for a few moments, waiting for the pain to subside. The doctor told me I shouldn't be bending or lifting, but thankfully the bag wasn't that heavy. Plus, it was huge, so it wasn't like I had to bend that far down to get it.

There was a card sticking out of a plastic holder. I weaved the handle of the bag through one arm as I held the card in the other.

It was an invitation with swirly cursive writing on it. *You are invited...* it said on the front. On the inside it said, *to dinner!* then Noland wrote *(for three!)* in parentheses with a smiley face.

His ass was really corny for this, but I couldn't front that it was also sweet.

The address to the location we were having dinner was at the bottom of the card, along with the time. My heart panged as I saw it was Ruth's Chris. The last time I had them was with Tray.

I shook that thought from my mind and entered my apartment, slipping off my shoes at the door. Then I walked over to the couch in the living room to look in the bag which held a sexy black dress, some lingerie, and heels.

"No, this nigga does not..." I started, but stopped myself. It had been a while. I hadn't had sex with Noland since that first time, so this was probably his way of asking me if I was ready.

I contemplated it.

Then I noticed another small box in the bottom of the bag. I opened it and there was a tennis bracelet inside. I didn't need to check it to know it was real.

My eyes filled with tears at my confliction.

One part of me was saying I was crazy as hell for still holding onto an inkling of Tray when I clearly had a whole other man, but another part of me was ashamed to admit that Noland didn't really do it for me.

"Maybe it's because you're not really giving him a chance," I said to myself.

I needed to make a decision, and now. Noland was getting serious about me, judging from this bracelet. It wouldn't be fair to string him along, accepting expensive ass gifts like this, just to turn around and leave him for Tray.

"Something's gotta give, Mia..."

I took a quick shower, then slid the dress on. It fit perfectly. I fixed my hair, which Becky had recently styled into a braided updo, applied some makeup, then I was on my way.

The restaurant was only a half hour away, and there was barely any traffic.

I pulled up right on time. I had decided to lock all of my thoughts of Tray into a little box in the back of my mind, and to throw away the key. As best as I could. I prayed and asked God for a sign that I was doing the right thing, then the restaurant doors opened and Noland stepped out dressed in a nice suit that went perfectly with my dress. He extended a single red rose toward me.

"Come on in, my lady," he said, then did a silly bow.

I giggled, then stepped forward to accept the rose and give him a hug. This man was too much.

We entered and were seated right away.

"How was your day?" Noland asked, and I assessed him before I responded, trying to see if I could really do this. He cleaned up really well, I could give him that. He was sweet, attentive, caring... He did all of this to make me feel comfortable. Make me feel good.

You're being an idiot, my mind screamed at me.

Before he could open his mouth to ask his question again, I cut in. "It was good. How was yours?"

He gave me a slow smile. "It was okay, but it's a lot better now."

The waitress came over and took our orders, then Noland filled me in on his day. He didn't do much but hit the gym after work, get my gifts, then take a nap, but I found myself listening intently anyway.

Then something dawned on me. "Noland, weren't you worried this bracelet could have gotten stolen? You did leave the bag right in front of the house."

He looked a bit embarrassed when I said that, then his face broke out into a grin. "Good thing no one got that idea," he said.

The waitress brought out our drinks first, then our food shortly after. Neither of us ordered appetizers, so our food came pretty quick.

"You look beautiful tonight," Noland commented after taking a sip of his water. Then he looked me up and down.

I took a bite of my steak. "Oh?" I shot him a coy glance of my own, letting him know I was open to whatever the night would hold for us. "Thank you."

Noland took the cue. He licked his lips. "Most definitely. I have a beautiful, sexy, intelligent woman sitting right across from me."

"Beautiful and sexy, huh?"

"Intelligent, too."

We stared at each other. Noland's gaze was unwavering, and I had to admit I felt his heat. It was time for me to be a grownup. Let Tray go, and embrace my new man.

His features shifted as he became more serious. "Mia..."

"What is it?" I took a sip of my lemon water.

He did the same before continuing.

"I want to ask you something."

My heart dropped. I couldn't tell if this was going to be a good or bad question. Was he worried I was still into Tray? Should I lie and tell him no?

Before my mind could continue its craziness, Noland stood, then knelt before me, holding out a ring box in a flawlessly executed fashion.

He held it out and opened it, with a tear in his eyes.

"I know it hasn't been that long for us, but I believe we're right for each other. How about we make things official? Will you marry me?"

Everyone's eyes were on us, including the waitress who had just come to ask us if we needed anything else.

An older lady was recording the interaction on her cell phone with a smile.

I had no choice.

Well, I did, but it felt like I didn't. *He's a good guy, Mia*...my mind told me.

"Yes!" I gushed, and Noland slid the ring on my finger amidst the applause of everyone seated around us.

Tray

I had to admit it felt good being a dad. At the same time, I didn't want to get too attached to Briella just in case she wasn't mine. I gave Loryn a few days because I felt like it would be an asshole move to ask for the DNA test the same day the baby was born.

I agreed to take pictures and let her post them on social media. If this little girl was mine, I wanted things to be right. I would never want her to think her daddy didn't love her or want her.

Granted, I didn't want a baby in this way, but still...

"Tray, can you bring me some pampers and wipes?"

Briella had just woken up after her two-hour nap and was ready to eat and be changed. I had sort of moved out of Ant's spot when she was born, sleeping on a sleeping mat in the nursery while Loryn slept in the bed with the baby.

We had a little spat about that when Loryn bought her home because I read online that you're not supposed to sleep with the baby in bed with you. Loryn cussed me clean out, and I snapped back and hurt her feelings.

"Whatever. It's your kid, anyway," I had said, but I didn't mean for it to come out like that.

She looked at me like I wounded her. "You still on that, Tray? When your daughter looks just like you?"

I didn't see any resemblance between me and the baby, but I kept my mouth shut. Plus, my mom was all excited about her first grandchild, and Loryn's mom, too. I wasn't about to get jumped by a pack of crazy females.

Especially since my mom already told me I was being immature.

Still, late at night I found myself going through my phone and looking at old pictures and videos of me and Mia. I had so many memories with that girl, and now it was over.

I didn't want to look at her social media because I would probably see pictures of that new nigga, but I missed her. We talked a few times a week because we possibly had our own baby on the way, too, but it wasn't the same.

I felt like Mia was tolerating me rather than having conversations. We were nothing like what we used to be.

"Why are you so spaced out?" Loryn asked when she finished changing Briella and handing me the dirty diaper.

I didn't respond. I went to throw it in the trash and wash my hands.

When I came back into the living room, Briella was already almost done with her bottle. "That girl can eat," I remarked.

"Just like her daddy," Loryn said with a smirk, and I felt sick to my stomach.

I didn't remember anything that happened that night, and I didn't care to. Hearing this new information made me die a little inside.

Loryn sucked her teeth just as Briella finished her bottle. Then she proceeded to rub and pat her back to get her to burp.

I couldn't front that it was a beautiful sight, but I was standing there looking stupid just watching. I sat on the loveseat away from the couch that Loryn and Briella were on.

"When you think you're going to be ready for the test?" I blurted out.

She shot daggers in my direction. "Why are you so concerned?"

"What do you mean, why am I so concerned?"

Briella finally burped, then Loryn placed her in her bassinet so she could go back to sleep.

"You keep asking me this every few days."

"It's not every few days, Loryn. The last time I asked was before the baby was even born."

Loryn turned to face me. "And she's been here for what? A week? If you don't want to be a father, just say that. I already got enough weight on my back."

Her eyes filled with tears, and I stepped back for a second.

"Look, Loryn. I'm not trying to add pressure on you, but we need to get this test sooner or later. It's not fair to me or any other potential father to go too far without the truth."

Loryn scoffed at my words. "Any other potential father? Tray, do you really think I'm a whore?"

When she asked that, I felt bad again. I couldn't keep hurting this girl's feelings. I was becoming a toxic nigga, and that ain't never been me.

"I'm not saying you're a whore. I don't think that at all. I just want to be able to have peace with the situation."

"What about us?"

I wasn't following. "What do you mean, us?"

"Are we going to try to forge a relationship?"

"You mean romantically?"

"Yes, Tray. Mia has moved on. I think you and I would work well together. We already are good at taking turns and everything with Briella, even though she's only been here a short time. Why don't we try it?"

I could tell she was sincere, but I was nowhere near ready to answer that kind of question right now.

"Let me think about it," I said instead.

Chapter 16: Mia

I fingered my engagement ring and it felt like deja vu. I was supposed to be stopping by Becky's salon for a few during my lunch break. My original plan was to tell her about Noland proposing, but now I wasn't so sure.

I entered the salon and was immediately proud of my friend. She had created a clean, friendly looking environment in such a short time. She already had two other stylists working with her and was planning to add a third in the near future.

"Hey!" she said, looking at me from behind the chair of the woman she was styling. It looked like she had a simple wash and blow dry with a little bit of curl to top it off.

"Look at you, Miss Thang," I said, walking over to give her a hug.

We embraced, then she stepped back to look at me. "Seems to me like you're the one who needs to be looked at. Don't think I didn't catch that big ass ring. How did he do it?"

I opened my mouth, but closed it. *Damn, she noticed that quick?*

"Girl, he took me to Ruth's Chris."

I told her about how I came home to the gift bag, and how Noland had set everything up so nicely. When I got to the part where he proposed, every woman in the room was oohing and awing.

"Why don't you look happy?" Becky asked.

"I am," I said, a little too quickly.

Her eyes narrowed. "I know you ain't still worried about…"

"I can't help it, Becky."

She continued her client's hair, then when she finished, I followed her to the cash register and watched her complete their transaction.

"Listen, Mia. You found true love with Noland. You need to hold onto that because so many women never find it."

Her words made me pause. I wasn't sure if they were true. I did like Noland, but I didn't feel like I loved him the same way I did Tray. At the same time, Becky and Loryn had cried on my shoulders many times about the no-good men they had dealt with. Here I was with a good man who was bending over backward for me. Maybe I was just being immature about this whole situation. Maybe I was being selfish. Greedy.

Here Noland was doing everything he could for me, and I was still fucked up over Tray when he went and fucked my best friend, not to mention getting her pregnant.

I needed to snap out of this shit. Quick.

Tray

Well, there's a shocker. I wasn't Briella's father.

Some people might find what I did fucked up, but I had to. Loryn had been dodging me for weeks about the DNA test, but at the same time, trying to get me to cozy up to the idea of us being together. I appreciated her efforts, and even felt guilty for constantly denying her, but just like women had intuition, niggas got it too.

Briella wasn't mine.

I ordered one of those home DNA kits online, took a sample from Briella while Loryn was asleep, and sent it in along with my own.

Now I had some information that I didn't fully know what to do with.

It said there was a zero percent chance I was the father, just like I knew it would, but now that I knew, I didn't know how I was going to break the news to Loryn.

I went through my work day nervous as hell. I tried to rehearse what I would say to Loryn the entire time, but I finally came to the conclusion that there wasn't a nice way to say it. The baby wasn't mine, and I was going for Mia full force.

I was pulling up to Loryn's house when I saw a nigga coming off her stoop. The same nigga I saw there before a few months back.

Who he was wasn't my concern since I was now scot-free, but I couldn't deny I was a little curious.

I approached him with peace to let him know I wasn't on no confrontation shit.

"Eyo, my man. What's good with you?"

He sized me up and realized I wasn't a threat, then extended his hand to dap me up.

"Ain't shit. Just leaving my baby mom's house."

The way he said that made everything come to me full force. Loryn was playing this nigga, just like she played me. She was so adamant about me being the father, but she was probably doing the same to this nigga.

I opened my mouth to tell him this, but he continued.

"I appreciate you stepping in while I'm at work, washing dishes and shit."

I stepped back. Oh, so this nigga thought I was actually the father, and he was fucking my girl. I didn't catch the sarcasm in his tone when he first said he was leaving his baby momma's crib, but now I realized he thought he was sonning me. Nigga was about to get a rude awakening.

"Looks like you about to have a whole lot more responsibility around here, my dude, 'cause this bitch ain't trapping me. I ain't the daddy."

I held out the DNA test for emphasis.

I couldn't help but smirk as I saw the wheels turn in his eyes, then the steam rise from his ears.

"Loryn!" he thundered loud enough for her to hear from inside the apartment.

I left the paper with him as Loryn came out the door looking bewildered. I saw him approach her with the paper in my rearview, but I didn't bother to stick around to watch their argument.

My work was done here. Time to get my baby back.

Chapter 17: Mia

I pulled into the driveway absolutely exhausted. Noland had just moved in last weekend, and it was an adjustment with us living together.

Not that we argued or anything, but it was weird having him there at night when we went to sleep, and still there when I woke up.

In addition, Noland had weird little mannerisms about him. Like for instance, he wiped his ass with a wet washcloth after taking a dump right before he went to work his third shift, then had my upstairs bathroom smelling like shit the next morning because he didn't empty the trash bin.

When I asked him about it, he said he forgot to take out the trash because he was running late.

"But why did you wipe your ass with the washcloth? There was plenty of tissue."

He looked at me funny.

"Oh, that's what I always do to speed up the process."

That was on our first official night together.

On Monday when I went to work and came home, my entire living room was rearranged. Noland had also put his graduation and baby pictures up on my walls, along with some of mine that he had taken from the dining room, and he took down the large photo I had of me and Tray.

I understood why he did that part, but it still rattled me. I tried to approach the subject lightly. "Did you get bored or something?" I gestured at the arrangement of the couches and TV, then I noticed the brand-new area rug he had put down.

Noland was barefoot and ashy, and he was in the middle of eating a huge mixing bowl full of Lucky Charms mixed with Coco Puffs with a serving spoon while playing a video game. He looked up at me.

"Hey, babe! How was work?"

He looked so happy to see me that I wasn't going to get on him about moving everything around.

"It was good. Hey, where did you put the picture of me and Tray? The big one that was on the wall?"

Noland shrugged and focused on his game. "Oh, I threw it out."

I froze. "You threw it out?"

His eyes were still glued to the screen.

"Yeah, I figured you didn't need it anymore. Plus, that would be a great spot for our wedding picture once we take one."

I couldn't argue with that, though my heart was definitely not ready to part with me and Tray's picture yet. Then I realized I was being stupid again. This was Noland's apartment just as much as mine. Why shouldn't he feel he had a right to move a few things around? It wasn't like it was a bad idea. The new placement of the TV actually blocked more of the sunlight from hitting the screen, and the area rug made the living room pop more. I was just being selfish. I needed to calm down.

Then he scared me.

Not like, afraid-for-my-life scared me, but he definitely scared me.

On Tuesday night, I was knocked out by nine in the evening, per usual, when I had the urge to pee around ten. I noticed Noland wasn't next to me in bed, but I figured he must have already left for work. I went to the bathroom, but when I came out, I heard him chuckling downstairs.

I went down to see what he was laughing at, and noticed he was watching something on TV. My entire body froze when I saw myself on the screen, in the kitchen, earlier that day.

I gasped, and he whipped his head around.

"Hey!" His eyes darted from me to the TV, then back again. He clicked it off. "Did I wake you?"

I wasn't letting him play this off. "Noland, do you have cameras in my house?"

He got up from the couch, and I took a step back up one of the stairs.

"Mia, it's not what you think. I just put a few around here and there for when the baby gets here."

My mind tried to process what he was saying. "Around here and there? Like around the house where?"

"Just the living room, kitchen..." he looked a little nervous. "The bathroom, stuff like that."

He tried to say the bathroom really quick so I wouldn't notice.

"Why do you have the cameras in the bathroom?"

He took another step toward me.

"It was just in case you slipped and fell and needed me or something. I have all the cameras connected to my phone."

He whipped it out for emphasis.

I felt the color drain from my face. This was a side of Noland I had never seen. A side I wasn't sure what to make of.

"Noland, why didn't you just get baby monitors if you wanted to look out for Junior? And why didn't you tell me you installed cameras everywhere?"

He shrugged. "I guess it slipped my mind. My bad."

I watched him as he went to grab his work vest, then put it on. He walked back over to me, clearly not noticing my apprehension.

"Get some rest. I'll see you in the morning."

Then he kissed me and walked out the door.

I shook myself out of my thoughts about the past few days with Noland as Tray's car pulled up behind me. It was then that I realized that I had been sitting in my car for over ten minutes.

I slid my engagement ring off my finger, then got out as Tray approached. I wasn't sure why I did that. I guess I just wasn't ready to tell him.

"Mia..." he looked nervous.

"What are you doing here, Tray?"

"Can I come in? We need to talk."

There was no way I could let him in without him noticing Noland now lived there. Matter of fact, Noland would probably be coming home from the gym any minute now. He texted me while I was on my way home from work saying that he stopped there to do a quick workout before I came home.

Gotta keep myself up for my baby, he sent along with sending a glistening photo of his abs.

"Mia?" Tray was adamant.

"No, Tray. You can't come in. What did you want to talk to me about?"

"Mia, Loryn's baby is not mine."

That hit me like a ton of bricks.

"What do you mean, she's not yours?"

My mind was fighting to grapple with this information while Tray continued the story. "I should have known from the beginning. I saw a nigga there a few months back, then I saw him again today when I went to give her the DNA results. He's probably the father."

I looked at Tray like he was speaking a foreign language. This was too much for me.

"Look, Tray, I don't know what to tell you. Apparently, Loryn is a hoe, but that's your problem. Take it up with your girlfriend."

I moved to walk away, but he grabbed my arm.

"She's not my girl, Mia. You are."

"No, I'm not. I have a whole other man in case you didn't remember." I hoped I sounded convincing when I spoke, but apparently, I didn't because Tray was still on it.

"Drop that nigga, Mia. Me and you can pick up where we left off."

"No, we can't, Tray. You still fucked her even if you're not the daddy. Plus..." My voice trailed off.

"Plus, what?" Desperation was written all over Tray's face.

Just then, I saw Noland's car coming down the street.

"Look, you gotta go. Like I said, I wasn't expecting you, and Noland is here."

"I don't give a fuck if that nigga is here. I..."

"Go, Tray!"

I could tell he was hurt by the way I said that, but I had to. This was all too much for me all at once.

Tray finally backed off. He got in his car while Noland waited for him to pull out so he could pull in. Thankfully, those two didn't exchange any words.

I turned and walked into the house, trying to look natural as I did. I had to get my ring back on so Noland wouldn't think anything.

Chapter 18: Mia

This revelation from Tray really threw me. Part of me was kicking myself for accepting Noland's engagement, but the other part of me remembered that Tray cheated.

I went outside in the morning to go to work and saw that my driver's side front tire was flat. "Ugh!" I said in frustration. That meant I would be late.

I contemplated asking Noland for a ride, but I didn't want him rushing to get to me since he wasn't home from his shift yet. Instead, I decided to catch an Uber.

Thankfully, there was one less than two minutes away, so I texted him after I got in the car to tell him about it.

Oh no! I could have brought you, he responded.

I'm good. Maybe you can pick me up when I get out.

Will do. And I'll take care of your car as well.

I smiled as butterflies swarmed my stomach. Noland was so sweet. I went through my day pretty smoothly. We were very busy so the hours flew by.

When I walked outside the building, I was pulling my phone out to call Noland to see if he was on his way and saw him pulling up.

I kissed him when I got inside. "Thanks, babe."

He smiled at me. "No problem."

We listened to music as we drove, but aside from some small talk, Noland was mostly silent, and then a little jumpy.

"What's up with you?" I finally asked.

He smirked. "Oh, nothing."

I knew he was up to something. "What is it?"

He stuck his tongue out. "Not telling."

I pretended to pout, but when we got to our apartment I saw that there was a different car parked where mine originally was this morning. A new car.

My jaw dropped. "What is this?"

Noland smiled in response.

"Noland, did you buy me a new car?"

His smile grew wider. "Something like that. I traded your old car in."

I was confused. "How were you able to do that without me being involved?"

He flipped his wrist like it was nothing. "Oh, easy. I gifted myself your old car, then traded it in and purchased the new car, then I gifted it back to you."

My head was spinning. "And how the hell did you do all this without any signatures or consents from me?"

Noland's smile vanished. "Are you upset with me?" He started stumbling over his words. "Oh no. I was just trying to help. Mia, I'm so sorry."

I could tell he was sincere, but Noland's behaviors were starting to get the best of me. "Noland, what did you do to get this car?"

He stared at me like he was afraid to continue, but he did. "I have a friend who is a notary. I saw your title in the drawer in the kitchen when I was looking for utensils, and that's when I got the idea. I have another friend who owns a dealership and he always tells me he can give me the hookup when I need it. I set this all in motion weeks ago, but I figured today was the perfect day to go ahead and get the new car since your old one was messing up."

I almost opened my mouth to tell him that my old car was not messing up. All it had was a flat tire, but I decided against it. Noland might have been weird as fuck, but I could tell he was trying to do something nice for me. Besides, the car was cute and it was a few years newer than my old car.

"This must have cost you a fortune," I said, lightening up my tone and getting out to look at the new vehicle.

Noland pulled my keys out of his pocket, but he did it like he was still unsure of himself. "They gave us two sets, but I figured I would keep one in case the first ones get lost or something."

I took the keys from him without saying anything. I noticed this one had a remote starter on it, which my old vehicle didn't have. "Thank you!" I said, and forced a smile. I was happy, seriously, but I was going to have to get used to the way Noland operated.

"It has heated seats, too," Noland said when he saw me playing with the remote start button. It started right away.

My heart warmed when Noland said it had heated seats. He must have done that because I complained a few times about running to the car in the winter time. I hated being cold. Now my reluctance was gone. "Thank you, babe," I said, and put my arms around his neck to pull him down for a kiss.

Tray

I knew Mia told me to leave her alone, and that she was with Noland now, but I felt like I was going crazy. Why did that nigga get to have my woman over some shit that wasn't even my fault?

Well, it was my fault since I slept with Loryn, but still. Damn, I wished I could turn back the hands of time.

I found myself scrolling social media while I was on my lunch break, looking again at all the old pictures and videos of me and Mia.

My heart burned as I realized how lost I was without her.

Our relationship was perfect... well, not perfect, but she was perfect for me. She kept me in check. She encouraged me on my goals. She's the one who helped me apply for my internships...Mia was everything to me. How could I cross her even if I was drunk? I must have been twisted as fuck that night, no lie. It wasn't the first time I blacked out and did some shit I didn't remember the next day, though.

The first time it happened was before I met Mia. It was the night my dad died. He had a rollover accident and died instantly on the scene. I felt like a piece of shit because he called me earlier that day, but I rejected it because I was trying to mack on some bitches. When I found out the news I broke down. Me and my dad weren't on the greatest of terms, but we did have a good relationship.

I couldn't help but to still feel guilty, though, so I got completely wasted that night. I woke up face down on

Trevor's living room floor. Him and Ant were sitting on the couch playing video games loud as fuck. It was a wonder that I was sleeping through it.

My head had immediately been filled with pain when I came to. "What the fuck happened?" I asked.

Ant answered. "Nigga, you was lit last night. We let you pass your limit because of what happened with your pops, but then you kept trying to drive so Trev knocked you out. I thought he broke your jaw."

That explained why my jaw was hurting. I thought it was because of my position on the floor.

I appreciated my friends that night because if it wasn't for them, I probably would have met the same fate as my dad. I guess I always been a little reckless.

I felt ashamed as I remembered those times. My mind flashed to my woman. Well, ex woman now. I went out of my page, then crept over to Mia's. I was thankful that she didn't block me yet. I wondered if she would if the baby wasn't mine. I prayed it was so I could still keep some type of contact with her.

That probably sounded weak as hell, but I needed her in my life.

Maybe there was still a chance...

Nope. She'd just updated her status to engaged.

Damn.

Right when I was walking back into the building from my break, Loryn called my phone.

"Fuck she want?" I said before answering. I didn't leave anything over at her house, so there was no need for us to be in contact.

"Hello?"

"Tray! Please don't hang up." Loryn sounded like she was in distress.

My mind flashed to the nigga I seen at her crib. I hope he didn't put his hands on her. Now I felt bad that I may have caused it by showing him the DNA results the way I did.

"What's wrong with you?"

She sniffled. "I just feel so horrible about what I did. I never meant to lie to you, but I really wanted you to be the father. I felt like we were made for each other."

I sighed. "Loryn, I'm sorry to hurt your feelings, but I'm not into you like that."

"Why not, though? Just give us a chance. Things aren't the same here without you."

"Loryn, I'm sorry. I can't help you. I gotta get back to work." I moved to hang up, but she was still talking.

"Tray, baby, please! Just give me a chance to prove myself. I promise you'll be happy with me. Briella is already attached to you, and I can't do this alone."

"What happened to your nigga?"

"Jermaine is a fucking deadbeat. He left that day you had the results. He was never gonna be there for her, anyway."

"Put him on child support."

She sucked her teeth. "I would if the nigga even had a job. He's not a real man like you, Tray. He's a bum ass nigga. You're what I need. My relationship with Jermaine was nothing but a mistake."

I was about to be late coming back from lunch. "Look, Loryn, I'm sorry you're going through it right now, but I really can't help you. I'm not Briella's father, and me and you were never in a relationship. What we did that night was a mistake."

"What if it was fate, though? What if it happened because we were meant to be?"

I stared at my phone. Either Loryn was still hormonal due to just giving birth, or her ass was crazy. I had time for neither.

"I gotta go," I said, and hung up before she could say anything else.

She tried to call me again immediately after but I declined it and turned off my phone.

Chapter 19: Mia

I was having a good ass sleep, which was getting harder and harder to do these days with my bump growing. Of course, while I was in the middle of my dead slumber, I had the urge to pee. I had been having the urge to pee throughout the night more and more the bigger this baby got.

I knew since I was nearing six months, this might be normal, but still.

I finally gave in and popped my eyes open, only to see Noland perched above me, staring directly into my face.

I was so caught off guard that I screamed and pissed myself at the same time.

"Oh my God, Noland!" I tumbled out of bed while he scooted back to his side. All types of thoughts were going through my mind. How long had he been in that position staring down at me? How come I didn't feel it? What the hell was going on with Noland?

"Mia, are you okay?" Noland looked worried.

"No, I'm not fucking okay!" It was no time for me to be nice now. "Why the hell are you staring down at me like that? You just made me pee the bed."

He chuckled. "No worries, mama. I'll clean it for you."

He flipped his nightstand light on and hummed as he removed our sheets and comforters, then brought them downstairs to the laundry room. I was so pissed I could barely function. I stomped over to the drawers to get a fresh pair of panties and more pajamas. Noland came back into the room just as I was exiting.

I didn't say one word to him as I brushed past, slamming the bathroom door as I went to take a shower.

While I was in there, I thought about if this was really what I wanted. It was clear by now that Noland and I were not compatible. He wasn't a bad guy, but he was way too much for me with the way he was acting.

I had removed the cameras that he put in the bathrooms after he told me about them, but since he acted so crushed, I let him keep the ones that were in the living room, kitchen, and nursery. He tried to fight me on the one he had in our bedroom, but I removed that one, too.

After my shower, I went back into our bedroom, where our bed was now freshly made with new sheets and a comforter. Noland was laying on the side I peed on.

I was half-disgusted, half-grateful, but I didn't let him onto either emotion.

"Hey," he said, but I got into the bed, turned to my side so I was facing away from him, and drifted back off to sleep.

The next morning, the situation was still bothering me, so I reached out to Becky. "Girl, long time no hear," she said when she answered.

"Bitch, shut up. I just talked to you the other day."

"Why you sound so cross?"

I sighed. "Becky, I don't think I can do this anymore."

Now she sounded concerned. "Do what anymore? What happened?"

"Noland." I told her about all the stuff he had been doing lately. It felt good to let it all out to someone, but I also felt kind of guilty because I knew in my heart, he had good intentions.

"Damn, Mia," she said when I finished. "I would say come over so we can have some drinks but you're pregnant."

"Thanks for reminding me." Tears rose in my eyes.

"Oh, no, I didn't mean it like that. Listen, why don't we hang out today when we get off work? You clearly need a moment away from Noland, and after that incident last night, he shouldn't mind."

"Psst, I don't care if his ass minds. I'm there."

Becky chuckled. "See you, babe!"

When I got off the phone with Becky, I texted Noland to let him know I was going over her house after work.

Oh, I didn't realize you were hanging out. I wanted us to have a talk tonight, he responded.

I scrunched up my face. *We can talk when I get home.*

He didn't fight me back with his reply. *Okay.*

As I was entering the building to begin my shift, Tray texted me. *Can we talk today? Please?*

I paused. I didn't really want to be around Tray while I was feeling so emotional. Last time I did, my ass came up pregnant. Still, I couldn't deny that I missed him. Tray might have fucked up, but when I was with him it felt natural. I truly believed we were made for each other.

I blinked back a tear and slid my phone into the front pocket of my purse. I had some thinking to do.

Work was quick, thank God, and I was back in the parking lot, leaving my job before I knew it.

My mind was on both Noland and Tray.

I put my blinker on and decided to see what Tray wanted to talk about.

I found myself sitting in the passenger seat of Tray's car outside his job. "What did you need to talk to me about?" I asked.

His eyes swept up and down my body. That used to make me swoon back in our day. I couldn't front. I was swooning a little now, at least internally.

"Mia, I need you."

Those words filled the air between us for almost a minute before I responded.

"Tray, I can't."

"I know you're engaged to him now." Tray's voice was hollow when he spoke those words. "But I can't help it, Mia. I feel like I'm going crazy."

That comment made me pause. Tray was spitting my life right now. I felt like I was going crazy without him, too. We were two peas in a pod. Why did life deal us a hand like this?

Then I snapped out of it. How quickly I kept forgetting that this nigga fucked my best friend. Well, ex best friend now, but still.

"Noland and I are getting married."

"Break it off. I already know you not really feeling the nigga."

My face grew hot. "And what makes you think something like that?"

Now he switched to a husky tone as he repositioned himself so that he was closer to me. "No nigga can make you feel like I do."

He was telling the truth about that but there was no way in hell I was letting it on.

"I have to leave." I moved to open the door, but he gently grabbed my wrist.

"Answer me this. Are you happy with him?"

"Yes." I spoke too quickly, and we both knew it.

"Happier than you were with me?"

I opened my mouth, then closed it. I couldn't let him win. I couldn't let him in again just to re-break my heart when I wasn't finished healing from the first time.

I removed my hand from his grasp. It was feeling way too tingly for my liking.

"I have to go."

This time, he let me. Part of me was glad about that, but the other part wished he tried harder.

Chapter 20: Mia

I was walking up the stoop to enter my apartment when I realized that I never met up with Becky. "Shit!" I pulled out my phone, and low and behold, she was calling me.

I went to answer it, but before I could, the front door wrenched open and Noland pulled me inside.

I let out a scream because he startled me, then another as I saw that he was wielding a hammer.

"Noland, what the hell!"

I dropped my phone on the floor, and as soon as Noland saw it, he snatched it up, held it against the wall, and banged on it repeatedly. His demeanor was so aggressive that I took a few steps back. There were veins popping out his neck. I didn't know what to do. This man literally just put a hole in my wall and shattered my phone into a million pieces. He still had the hammer in his hands when he turned back to me.

His eyes were blazing.

"You went to that nigga's job?"

Before I could process what he was saying, he took a step closer, and I took another one back, almost tripping over the edge of the area rug.

"Noland, calm down. How did you even know I was at Tray's job?"

"I have tracking on your car, Mia. I put it on there to make sure I could always find you in case you needed me, but when I checked it today, I see that you are with Tray? How could you betray me like that?"

This was too much for me. The hammer, the cameras, and now a damn tracking device on my car? I suddenly didn't give a fuck that this nigga had a weapon. Boldness grew within me. Or stupidity, but I wasn't dealing with this shit anymore.

"Get the hell out of my house."

Noland looked taken aback as he calmed. "What do you mean, get out?"

"I wasn't cheating on you with Tray, Noland."

"You told me you were going to Becky's."

"And I was, but then Tray said he had to meet with me."

"For what?"

"It doesn't matter for what. We're done. I can't do you anymore. All this shit you have going on, it ain't for me."

He dropped the hammer. "Mia, you can't mean that."

"Oh, but I do. I don't know if it's counseling or whatever that you need, but you don't need to be in a relationship with me."

Noland's eyes were all over the place, which was scary in itself, but I stood my ground, not giving an inch in my demeanor. Finally, a tear slid down his cheek. "What about the baby?" He looked so dejected, I almost felt bad but I maintained my stance.

"We'll cross that bridge when we get there."

Chapter 21: Mia

Twins. Oh my God.

I should have known my belly was growing way too big, despite the fact that I was coming up on six months. I felt like I was eating for three rather than two with the way I had been chomping down on everything I could see like it was nobody's business, but now it was confirmed.

"Shocked?" the ultrasound technician said with a smile. I didn't even know how to respond to her.

Apparently, I had two baby boys growing inside of me. The other one must have been hiding during the first ultrasound I had.

I felt like a deflated balloon.

The more I tried to understand what the hell was going on with my life, the more confusing it became.

God must hate me.

I left that appointment with my mind completely blank. I trudged toward my car, but stopped as I noticed this vehicle moving way too fast trying to get the parking spot that was just beyond me. I waited for them to go by since apparently their appointment was so much more important to them than a pregnant woman who was trying to get to her car.

Suddenly, I felt someone roughly push me from behind.

I was caught completely off guard, so my hands reached out, but I still fell right in line of the approaching vehicle.

"Oh my God!" I screamed, and my life flashed before my eyes. I felt the bumper hit my shoulder, then I was jerked onto my back from the impact. It all happened so fast.

I squeezed my eyes shut because I just knew that this was the end and that this car was going to roll right over me. Right over me and my babies.

It didn't.

The driver apparently slammed on his or her brakes because the steam that I felt blowing into my face from the undercarriage of the car was no longer there. The driver reversed a little.

I heard voices all around me. *"Oh my God, is she okay? Oh my God, did you see that? Move! The EMT's are coming!"*

I kept my eyes closed the entire time because this couldn't be life.

I finally opened when I heard someone calmly ask, "Miss, are you awake?"

I was staring up at a young white man wearing an EMT uniform. I nodded and swallowed back my tears.

"This is the second time they tried to kill me," I croaked.

"Huh?" he asked, looking confused, then he continued his inspection of my body.

Shortly after, I felt myself being lifted up onto a stretcher and loaded into an ambulance, then they drove me around to the other side of the hospital where the emergency room was.

Thankfully, aside from a dislocated shoulder from where the car hit me, and a back sprain from the impact, me and my babies appeared to be okay.

I called Noland and Tray back to back to tell them I was in the hospital and had been pushed in front of a car.

Of course, they both said they were on their way immediately.

The doctor said he wanted to monitor me overnight, however, then the police walked in.

Apparently, the EMT had alerted the authorities about my comment that this was the second time someone tried to kill me.

At first, I was going to voice my concerns, then I decided against it. I had no idea if the two incidents were truly connected. The only thing I knew was that one involved a car that almost hit me, and the other involved someone pushing me in front of a car.

"Unfortunately, no one was able to identify the individual who pushed you in front of the vehicle. The driver of the car saw the incident, but the only description that he gave was that the person was wearing all black."

I snorted in response to that.

"Miss Bradley, are you sure you have no idea who could have done this? Any suspicious behavior from any friends? A boyfriend? Coworker?"

Actually, I had all three of those, but I wasn't sure if any of them would do something like this. From what I gathered, Loryn was just a hating bitch. I didn't peg her as the type who would try to kill me. Noland was crazy, but I really didn't get the killer vibe from him, despite the incident with the hammer, and the only coworker I had issues with was Evelin, but her ass was happy in her supervisor position now.

"No, I don't."

He looked like he didn't believe me.

"Here's my card if you happen to remember anything."

As soon as he exited, I remembered those random ass emails and texts I was getting before. My breath caught in my throat. Could this all be related?

I didn't have too much time to think about it because Noland and Tray came rushing into the room.

"Mia, are you okay?" Noland asked. His tone of voice and facial expression were frantic, and his eyes looked like he felt guilty that this happened.

Tray was assessing me with tears in his eyes. "Baby..." he said in a low, gravelly voice.

"She's not your girl!" Noland said, stepping toward me like he was trying to protect me from Tray.

I gave him the side eye. His ass was the one with a whole hammer the other day. I hoped he didn't think I forgot that, much less the fact that I broke up with him.

I took control of the room. "Look, I didn't call y'all here to argue about who I'm going to be with. I had you come to tell you that I'm having twins."

Stunned silence filled the room.

"Are you serious?" Tray said first. He looked like he wanted to touch me, but was holding himself back.

Noland, however, didn't get the memo that I wanted this to be a peaceful situation. "Yes, she's serious. We're having twins. Now, you can pay child support if you like and have visitation if they're yours, but Mia and I are moving forward."

Before Tray could answer, I cut in.

"Noland, back the fuck away from me please. Do I need to remind you that I broke up with you? We're not together anymore. You can keep your ring."

"Mia, you can't be serious. Over one little incident?"

My eyes practically popped out of my head. "One incident!" Before I could continue, I felt this horrible strain in my stomach. I lost my breath.

"Ughhhh!" I grunted, and I felt a little dizzy.

Noland and Tray called for the nurse.

She examined me as the painful feeling subsided. I told Noland and Tray to leave. "I can't deal with y'all right now."

Thankfully, they did. Before they left, however, Tray told me to call me if I needed him, and of course, Noland repeated the same.

What the hell did I get myself into?

Tray

I felt like I had to do something, but I didn't know
what. The only thing I knew was that I was ready
to fight for what was mine.

I texted Mia later on that night to apologize for
getting into it with Noland while she was in the hospital,
and she accepted. Then I asked her if she wanted me to
drive her home in the morning when they discharged
her.

At first, I thought she was gonna say no because an
entire hour passed before she responded, but in the end
she agreed. Thank God.

I wondered why she broke up with the Noland dude,
especially since they just got engaged, but no way in hell
was I rocking the boat by asking.

If she didn't mention it, I wouldn't either. I would
just take it as a sign that there was still a chance for us.

The next morning, I got to the hospital bright and
early and was pissed off to see Noland in her room sitting
by her bedside.

He immediately tensed when he saw me too, but
neither of us said anything.

I could tell by his demeanor that he was trying to stay
on her good side, too. Fuck this nigga. If he thought he
could compete, he could go head and try.

Me and Mia had longevity. Him and Mia ain't have
shit. The best he could say was that they had a one-night-
stand that lasted too long.

Of course, I didn't know that for sure, but from my observations, she was nowhere near as into him as she was into me.

All I needed was one more chance to make this right.

"Okay, Noland," Mia said. "Tray is gonna take it from here."

"He's taking you to our house?"

"Our house?" I shot back. "My name ain't off the lease yet."

If looks could kill, I would have been a dead man. Noland didn't respond. Probably still trying to win her back.

The nurse came with the discharge papers, and another one came with a wheelchair.

"I'll push it," Noland offered, but the nurse explained that it was the hospital's policy to have an employee do it.

We got outside the hospital and I pulled up my car.

Noland was standing there glaring at me with his hands in his pockets. I knew he wanted to say some shit, but he was holding back due to Mia.

Damn, he really cares for her, I thought, but it wasn't my problem. Mia was my woman. Fuck this nigga.

When Mia and I got in the car, we drove in silence at first, then I broke the ice because I just couldn't help but to ask. "You really done with Noland?"

She nodded. "He was starting to scare me, Tray."

My grip on the steering wheel tightened. "Scared you how?" *I swear, if this nigga ever put his hands on her...*

"Not like that," she said, putting her hand on my shoulder as she noticed my reaction. "He would just do weird little things."

"What kinds of things?"

She began to describe it to me, and I agreed that this nigga was crazy as hell. "I want to stay with you tonight," I declared.

She opened her mouth to protest, but I clarified.

"Not like that, but just as a precaution. The doctor says you gotta be on partial bed rest anyway, right? Until the babies come?"

She nodded, then stared at her hands.

It broke my heart to see her so emotional.

"Hey," I reached one hand over to touch hers, making sure I kept one eye on the road as well. "We gonna get through this, Mia. For real."

Those words seemed to calm her. "Thanks, Tray."

When we pulled up to the house, I looked over and saw a tear sliding down Mia's cheek. "What's wrong?" I asked as my heart panged.

"How did we get here?"

I didn't have a response for that, seeing that it was all my fault.

"I swear, Tray, I wish I had a time machine. If I did, I would erase all this shit and not even have fought with you the night you slept with Loryn."

"It's not your fault. I should have stayed home with you and discussed the situation like a man instead of going out to party."

She turned to look at me. "Has Loryn tried to contact you since she found out you're not the father?"

I nodded. "Yeah, she's still trying to kindle a relationship, but I only have room for one woman in my heart. That's you."

We were silent again after that, then I grabbed her purse and helped walked her into what used to be our apartment.

We chilled and watched TV all day, binge watching our favorite shows like we used to.

The next morning, I got a bright idea.

"Mia, what if the twins are mine? Do you think we could put all this behind us?"

She took a moment to think before responding. "We could try."

Those words encouraged me more than she could ever know. "Why don't we get an early DNA test? Can we do one before the babies are born?"

She looked at me like that thought never occurred to her. "Damn, that's a good idea. I wonder if it's possible."

She whipped out her phone and called her primary care right then and there.

Unfortunately, he called back an hour later to say that a prenatal DNA test could be done if there was one fetus, but not multiples.

"Damn, back to square one," I said, staring at the calendar on the kitchen wall as if my eyes could will the dates to move faster.

I was off that day, so I stayed with Mia again. I was trying to soak up this time with her the best I could. If she didn't tell me to go, I wasn't planning on leaving.

I had to work the next day, however. I would have called out, but Mia promised she would hit me if she needed me, and plus her mom and Becky were coming by to check her as well.

When I pulled up to the building where my job was located, Loryn was standing there with a crazed expression on her face.

Maybe not a crazed expression, but she was definitely out of her mind for clocking my moves like this.

"Shit," I said to myself, praying internally that she didn't cause a scene. I got out of the car and approached her because there was no way to get in without her seeing me.

"Shouldn't you be at home with Briella?" I asked.

"My mom is watching her." Loryn looked me up and down.

"What is it?" I was losing patience already. "I have to get to work, and you really shouldn't be coming to my job like this."

"Why won't you answer my phone calls?"

"Because we have nothing to say to each other."

"Why not, though?"

"Loryn, I think you should see a doctor or something. You are so fixated on the idea of us being together but I keep telling you I'm not interested."

"Tray..."

"No. I'm trying to be cordial about it, but I'm running out of nice ways to break it off to you. For the very last time, what happened between us was nothing but a mistake. I'm not the father of your baby, and I think you should pursue that Jermaine nigga rather than me. He was clearly feeling you based on his reaction to the DNA test."

"Fuck that nigga!" she spat just as one of my coworkers was walking in. Sally turned to look at our exchange.

"Everything okay?" she asked.

I smiled and pretended it was. "Oh yes, I was just about to come in."

Sally nodded and walked into the building. I moved to follow her, but Loryn grabbed me.

I pulled my arm away. "Please don't come here anymore. I could get fired with you out here cussing and shit like you have no sense."

"But Tray..."

"No buts. Leave me alone, or I'm filing for harassment."

That seemed to make her snap out of it, at least for now. She walked toward the parking lot, so I went in.

My shift flew by, mostly because my mind was on getting back to see Mia, but when I exited the building and went to my car, I saw that Loryn had keyed it. She put *L+T* inside a big ass heart on the passenger side front door. At first, I was pissed as hell and was ready to call her phone and cuss her out, but I decided against it. It would probably only bring more drama.

Chapter 22: Mia

I woke up to another email message from a random address like the others. *You lucky, bitch. Almost got you. Next time, I won't miss.*

Judging from that, I was correct to assume that all of these random incidents were related. Why, though? Why wouldn't the person just show their face?

I was sick of this shit.

I never asked to be targeted, and I swore I had never done anything to anyone that would warrant this type of treatment.

Apparently, that didn't matter to whoever this was.

Becky decided to stop by to sit with me for a second before she went into her salon. Thankfully for her, business was booming. She now had a full set of stylists offering every different type of hair style a person could think of, along with lashes, and she was getting her nail and lash tech licenses in the near future. I was beyond proud of my girl, for real.

"Look at you, Miss Oprah!" I said when she entered my apartment. We hugged.

Becky blushed. "Girl, you tried it. I'm just glad you convinced me to finally step out there." We made our way to the couch. "When is Noland coming to get all his stuff?"

Suddenly I felt a little nervous. I hadn't told Becky about me and Tray possibly rekindling our relationship. She had blown a gasket a while back when she found out I slept with Tray, and I didn't think I could deal with the stress of her knowing now.

No, I told myself, shaking my head. I would have to see how things went with Tray on my own.

"Hello? Earth to Mia!" Becky was waving her hand in front of my face.

I blinked. "Oh, girl. My bad. He's supposed to be coming this weekend, but he keeps stalling."

"Hmph." She stared at me like she wanted to say something.

"What is it?"

"Mia..." Her voice trailed off.

"What is it, Becky?"

"Why did I see Tray's car here last night?"

"What do you mean, last night?"

She crossed her arms. "I was going to come see you after I left the salon to make sure you were good, but when I saw his car, I decided against it. Are you guys back together?" She looked so disappointed in me. It broke my heart.

"Becky..."

"Don't tell me that's what it is, Mia."

I sighed. So much for trying to process it myself. "Look, Becky. I'm doing the best I can right now. All this came to me out of nowhere. I had no idea Tray was cheating on me, then I meet Noland, then I get pregnant, and it's all just too much. I need space and time to make my own decisions. I can understand you are trying to be my friend, but I just can't argue with you about this right now."

Now, Becky was the one that looked hurt by my outburst.

Her eyes filled with tears. "Mia, I just don't like seeing you like this. I'm sorry if it seemed like I was judging you. It's just that I've been trying to be there for you but it feels like you are shutting me out."

At that moment I understood where she was coming from.

"I'm sorry, girl. I didn't mean to make you feel that way." I reached out to touch her arm and her features softened.

"But I will say this one thing, though..." Becky stared at me like she was unsure whether to continue. "I would be leery about staying with Tray. I know that's not what you want to hear right now, but if he did it once, he could do it again."

At first, I was going to respond to Becky's comment, but I decided to leave it alone. We never knew what the future might hold.

Chapter 23: Mia

Giving birth was single handedly the hardest thing I ever went through. The pain was absolutely crazy, but thank God my labor was only three hours. Hopefully that meant these babies were going to be easy to deal with.

From what I heard, boys were quite the handful, and I had two of them. Tyreik and Tyrell. Noland had wanted a junior and I told him I might consider changing one of their names if he was the father, but I would have to deal with that when the time came.

Thankfully, he didn't fight me on that, but that was just about the only thing.

Pushing the boys out was hard enough, but what made matters worse was Noland and Tray. I swore, those two were trying to be the death of me.

Even though Tray and I were taking things slow, Noland kept trying to butt back into my life. He finally came and got his stuff after about two weeks of stalling, but it didn't matter because he was always calling and texting me, sending me gifts and flowers, trying to get me to leave Tray for good and go back with him.

I meant what I said earlier, though. I couldn't do Noland's personality.

On the day the babies were born, he was sitting there yelling in my ear trying to help me push because he went to Lamaze classes on his own after I decided to do mine with Tray. His ass looked ridiculous. Even the doctor laughed.

I got that he was trying to prove himself, but in my opinion, there was nothing to be proven. I made my choice, and I chose Tray.

The tip of the iceberg that day was Noland pulling out his baby pictures after the babies were swaddled. He kept holding them up to each boy's face and declaring that he was definitely the father. I had to admit, they did kind of look like him, but they could also be seen as Tray's kids. I'd seen enough episodes of *Paternity Court* to know that it could really go either way.

I was originally going to wait a few weeks to send off for the paternity results, but I decided to send them off before we left the hospital instead. Tray and I were praying he was the father, and not Noland, so we could finally pick up where we left off with a clear mindset.

This whole damn situation was a mess.

Chapter 24: Mia

Tray and I had been with the boys nonstop since they were born. It had been a couple of weeks, but it felt like the time was flying. Noland wanted to move back in until the DNA results came, but I drew the line.

"Those are my kids, too, Mia!" he said with a pained expression on his face.

"We don't know that yet, Noland."

He sucked his teeth. "That's not fair that you're pushing me out of their lives already. If you don't want to be with me, that's fine, but don't forget this nigga is the one that cheated on you, not me."

I was so over him at that point. I snorted. "Yeah, he might have cheated, but you can't forget you came at me with a whole hammer."

"I did not…" he started, but I held my hand up to stop him.

"I'm not letting you stay here, and that's final. You and Tray have been at each other's throats for the past few months. I get that you want to be in your children's lives, and you will be, but as of right now, everything is pending these results. You can stop by, but you can't stay."

When I said that, he looked like he wanted to fight me on it so bad, but thankfully, he conceded. His shoulders slumped. "Okay, Mia. Sorry I couldn't make you happy."

I didn't know what he meant by that, but I left it alone.

Tray was out grabbing some more pampers at the time. Neither of us realized that Noland was already on his way with some, along with wipes. I had to admit, Noland might have been a little crazy, but he went hard for his sons.

His sons. Look at me already drinking his Kool Aid.

"Ugh, I can't wait til these results come in!" I said to Tray when he returned. He had a serious expression on his face. "What's wrong?" I asked.

That was when I noticed he was holding an envelope. My eyes widened. "Is that it?"

He nodded, his expression stoic.

I knew we were both thinking the same thing. He put the bag of diapers on the kitchen counter, then returned to the living room where I was with our sleeping infants. Tyreik was in a bassinet, while Tyrell was in a rocker.

Tray licked his lips, then swallowed as he clutched the envelope with nervous hands.

"Sit down. You're making me nervous, too," I urged him.

He sat next to me. "You open it. I can't see it if they're not mine."

I took it from him, holding the thin, white rectangular object like it was a bomb. For us, it was. This would determine how the rest of our lives, or at least the rest of our relationship, would go.

"Tray, what are we gonna do if..." I found myself getting choked up.

"We have to cross that bridge when we see it," he said. Tray was staring straight ahead with his fists balled like he was bracing himself.

I decided to do it quickly. I swiped open the envelope and unfolded the results page. My eyes scanned what it said and my heart dropped.

I didn't even need to tell Tray, but I did. "Noland," I got out before I choked up again.

A tear rolled down Tray's cheek. "Damn," he finally spoke. "I really wanted them to be mine."

He took the results from me and read them himself. "How come Tyrell is not on here?"

I hadn't even noticed that. I shrugged. "Maybe they send them separate since it's two different children?"

The color drained from Tray's face. "You don't think it's possible..."

I shook my head. "No. I'm pretty sure that's not possible."

But it was. The next day, the second envelope came. Tyrell was Tray's, according to that set of results.

I had a set of twin boys, with two different fathers. This could not be life.

Tray

I felt numb. Me and Mia were almost on our way, but now we were stuck with Noland for life. I was happy that at least Tyrell was mine, but it was weird as hell that someone could actually have twins by two different fathers. When we saw Tyrell's results, we weren't expecting that at all. We thought it wasn't possible, but when I called my mom and told her about it, she acted like it was common knowledge.

"Boy, you ain't never watched Maury?" she asked.

"Not really."

I watched as a car pulled up in the parking lot of my job. I was sitting outside on the front steps during my break.

"It's definitely possible. What are you and Mia gonna do?"

I opened my mouth to answer her, but Loryn was approaching me with that same crazed expression on her face she had the day she keyed my car.

"Ma, I gotta go," I said, and disconnected the call before she could ask what was wrong.

I stood from my seat as Loryn approached. This was my first day back, since Paternity Leave was some bullshit.

"You owe me at least five hundred dollars for keying my car," I declared.

She just stared at me before speaking. "Tray, we need to talk."

"About my money?" I was already sick of this girl, but I had to admit, the fact that the expression on her face hadn't changed as she spoke was worrying me. *Is she on drugs?* I thought, then I shrugged it off. Drugs or not, Loryn was no longer my problem.

She spoke up. "Why do you keep denying our love?"

I sucked my teeth. "Love? What the hell are you talking about? Loryn, we never had anything that even resembled love. You fucked me while I was drunk and thought you were Mia. Then you kept the baby instead of just getting an abortion. Claimed you wanted me so bad, while the whole time you were still fucking that nigga Jermaine, then you want to still try to trap me up even though I ain't the father because he turned out to be a deadbeat."

Loryn looked like she hadn't heard a word of what I said. Her expression was still as blank as it was when she first walked up to me. Her lips were slightly parted, and her hair was unkempt.

Finally, she spoke again. "Tray, we love each other."

"No. I think you need to set up an appointment or something because this is not a good look for you. Where is Briella, anyway?"

Finally, her expression changed, at least partially. She smiled. "Why don't you come by and see us?"

I shook my head, then glanced at my wristwatch. "Look, I gotta go back to work. Please don't come to my job anymore."

"Tray!"

"Make better decisions, Ma."

She was still calling my name as I jogged up the rest of the steps to get into my job, but I ignored her. I prayed I wouldn't walk outside to see four flat tires or no shit like that. I already had enough problems having to share one of my kids with Noland.

Thankfully, when I got off, Loryn was gone and my car appeared to be intact. I still had to get the paint job redone to fix where she keyed it, but I didn't have time to deal with it at the moment.

I called Mia on my Bluetooth.

"Hey," she answered. Something about the softness of her voice made me brick up. It was sexy as hell seeing Mia be a mom. Her little belly was starting to go down since she was eating as healthy as she could and sneaking in a workout or two here and there, but she was mostly tired all the time.

I kept telling her she was beautiful, but she still felt self-conscious. "What's up?"

She sniffled, and that put me on alert.

"What's wrong?" My mind immediately went to Noland. He had been stressing her lately, coming over every single day. Granted, the nigga did have a baby at the house, but I couldn't help feeling annoyed whenever he was around.

"Tray, do you think I'm a whore?"

"No," I said without hesitation. "I'm the one who put you in this predicament. If I had never gone out that night fucking around with Trev and Ant, we wouldn't be here. We would probably be married by now."

I felt myself choke up at that last part. It was true. Before all this happened, I had proposed to Mia. My daydreams about our life together turned into nightmares when Loryn told me she was pregnant.

I would probably never forgive myself for that shit.

I hung up with Mia as I pulled up to the apartment, and thankfully, Noland's car wasn't there. "Did he stop by?" I asked Mia after I gave her a hug and kiss.

She closed the door and locked it. "Not yet. He probably will in a few."

I fought the urge to roll my eyes, licking my lips instead. "The boys sleep?"

She eyed me. "Yeah, why?"

I stepped closer to her so I was up on her. I wrapped my arms around her again and looked into her eyes, letting my gaze linger.

She knew what I wanted.

"Tray, I'm still fat."

"Looks juicy to me."

She blushed. "That doesn't help."

"How about this?" I cupped her chin and kissed her slowly and sensually, like I used to do. At first, she remained tense, then she relaxed into me. Pretty soon, I was moving down to her neck and she was moaning.

"Tray..."

I lifted her up by the back of her thighs in response.

My fingers found their way around the front of her panties since that was all she was wearing underneath her robe. I held her up against the wall as my fingers continued to work their magic. Her lashes fluttered and her breathing became labored.

"It might not be time," she said, her face flushed.

"It's six weeks to the day," I reminded her. "I've been counting down."

Chapter 25: Mia

I woke to a three-paragraph rant in my text messages from Noland, cussing me out about fucking Tray while his baby was right there sleeping. Apparently, I had missed one of his cameras when I got rid of the others. I had no idea why he was still watching us. His ass was crazy. I was sick of it.

Becky decided to come see me during her lunch break. Tray was back to work now, and I only had a month left myself before I had to make a decision. Put my babies in daycare, or quit my job.

Tray said he would work and I could quit, and of course Noland was down for the cause, but I didn't want to lose my independence. I never envisioned myself as a housewife, though I could see how it made sense.

Plus, if it really wasn't for me, I could just go back to work once the babies were old enough for school...

Damn, I was really a mom.

"Hello! Earth to Mia!" Becky snapped her fingers in front of my face.

"What's up?" I said, coming back to our conversation.

Becky shot me a fake-stank look. "Whatever, girl. I'm not hurt that you don't care what's going on with my business."

Now I felt bad. "Becky, I'm so sorry I spaced out. What's going on with your business?"

"Monica."

"What did she do?"

"The bitch is doing way too much. She's mad that I'm blossoming, so she's creating fake accounts to leave bad reviews for me on all my social media sites, trying to make my ratings go down. Her ass is so dumb that she can't even spell, though. Plus, all her reviews keep saying the same thing over and over again. It's just a big mess." Becky leaned forward, resting her forehead on her palms as she tried to decide what to do about her former friend.

"Girl, I wouldn't even worry about Monica. Has business slowed?"

She looked back up at me. "Not really. I actually got a few new clients. I'm not sure if they initially came to gossip or what, but they walked out singing a different tune than the one they came in with."

I was so proud of my friend. "Girl, then you have your answer! Don't worry about Monica. She's gonna get what's coming to her. Any time you do someone wrong, that doesn't do wrong to you, you reap what you sow, honey."

Becky spaced out for a second, then she came to. "I guess you're right." She shrugged. "Anyway, what's up with you? Did they finally send y'all results yet?"

Damn. I felt like I fell right into that one. Of course, Tray and I got the results weeks ago, but I had been dodging Becky's questions about it. I didn't want to hear her mouth about what I should do.

I knew that probably sounded fucked up, but still. Becky could be a lot at times.

"Mia..." She looked suspicious.

"Ugh..." I squared my shoulders. "Okay, so we got them."

Her eyes were filled with intrigue. "And?"

"They're both the fathers."

She gasped, and I looked away to try to hide my embarrassment. I knew Tray was putting it on himself, but I was the one who slept with both of them the same day. He shouldn't have cheated, but I never should have fucked with Noland knowing I was in a vulnerable state. Now look at me.

"Mia, how is that even possible?" Becky asked.

See, this was why I didn't want to tell her. Her tone was already rising in octaves. Becky was going to blow her lid. I knew that from the beginning.

Thankfully, Tyriek woke at that exact moment, ready to eat. I had never been more grateful for a screaming infant. Instead of answering Becky's question, I rushed over to pick him up and feed him.

Becky fixed the bottle of formula for me. Pretty soon, Tyrell would be waking, too. They served as each other's little food timers. It was so cute.

"Can stuff like that really happen?" Becky asked again.

I sighed. "Apparently." I knew my word came out with attitude, but she needed to get off my back. I was already condemning myself every other day. I didn't need it from Becky too.

"Which one is Tray's and which one is Noland's?"

I focused on Tyriek's face as I spoke. He was chugging down his bottle like it was nobody's business. "Tyriek is Noland's and Tyrell is Tray's."

"Damn, Mia. At least you can tell them apart, seeing that they are fraternal."

I didn't respond.

Becky chuckled. "Tyrell is a little cuter, though."

I could tell she was just trying to lighten the mood, but I was not here for it. "Don't compare my babies' looks. Please and thank you."

Becky cocked her head. "Damn, well excuse me."

We heard a knock at the door. "Who is that?" I asked, sucking my teeth. Becky went to answer it. "Mia Bradley?" I heard an unfamiliar male's voice say.

Becky looked confused. "She's right over there."

He peeked his head in the door and waved. "May I come in, Ma'am?"

I slammed Tyriek's empty bottle down on my coffee table and walked over to him.

"Who the hell are you?"

He handed me a white envelope. "You've been served." He walked away.

My mind was swimming. "I've been served? What the hell?"

Becky took it from me. "It looks like it's from the courts. Noland?"

I felt my pressure rising. "It better fucking not be." Tyriek must have sensed my irritation because he started crying again.

Becky opened the envelope and scanned the summons. "He's going for full custody."

"That motherfucker!" I almost dropped my baby I was so mad. Then Tyrell woke up and started wailing. Now I had two screaming infants on my hands. Thankfully, Becky rushed over to feed Tyrell while I went back to the couch to change and rock Tyriek, and to calm myself.

Noland was starting to be a real fucking problem.

Tray and I were going to have to figure out how to get rid of him.

Chapter 26: Mia

When Tray came home, I was on ready. "We have to get rid of this nigga, babe."

He gave me a puzzled look. "Noland?"

My eyes filled up for the thousandth time that day. "Yes!" I thrust the paper in his direction.

Tray took it. "What is this?" he asked before reading it over. When he finished, he was silent for a second. "What do you wanna do, Mia?"

"We have to do something! He can't just take my baby. I'm the one who held him in my womb for nine months. Noland has absolutely no basis for trying to go for full custody. All because I moved on? What the hell?"

Tray put the paper down and stepped toward me, gently grabbing my elbows. "Listen, Mia. We're gonna get through this. Noland is not gonna take Tyriek."

I choked up. "How do you know that, though?"

"You're the mother. Don't courts always side with y'all, anyway?"

That made me feel slightly better. I took care of these babies every single day. There was no reason to remove either of them from our home. I nodded, finally feeling myself relax.

Tray cooked dinner while I tended to the boys. After we ate, we fed and changed the boys once more.

I took note of the perfect harmony Tray and I worked in. I thanked God I still had him, despite everything that happened over the past year or so.

The next morning, we had my mom watch Tyriek and Tyrell while Tray and I went down to the police station. "Y'all need to hurry back, though because I have somewhere to be tonight," she had said as we were walking out her door.

"Where do you have to be?" I asked her.

She pursed her lips.

"Mind ya business."

"Mm hm," I said. From the look in her eyes, I could tell she had a date.

"Tell me all about it tomorrow."

She smiled. "I will. Hurry back, please."

Tray and I left for the station. "We need to file a restraining order," I said when the clerk asked me what we were there for.

"Can you describe the situation? Why do you feel that this individual is a threat?"

When she said those words, I froze up. What could I really say?

Tray cut in. "Ma'am, this guy has been coming to our house every single day. He's had cameras installed without my fiancée's permission. He put a tracker on her car."

The clerk looked bored. "Has he issued any verbal or physical threat?"

At that moment, I wanted to talk about the hammer, but I didn't want to lie on Noland. He didn't actually try to hit me with it, though I said he did before. "He broke my phone," I offered instead.

She shot us a thin-lipped smile. "That might help, but you will probably need something more substantial, especially since you said he used to live in your house. Him installing cameras could be seen as something that was within his rights. Has he ever directly threatened you with violence or made you fear for your life?"

I felt myself getting frustrated. He couldn't win this. "No, but I just want him away from me."

"What about him damaging her property, though?" Tray tried again. "Her cell phone was her way of contacting someone if she needed help."

The clerk smiled at Tray. "Again, sir. His destruction of her property would have had to be attached to some kind of threat. You can certainly sue him for damages, and you can go ahead and file for the restraining order anyway, but you might just be wasting your time."

So basically this nigga could do whatever he wanted to us, and as long as he wasn't deemed a threat by the courts, it was whatever.

I never felt so powerless in my life.

"What, do they just wait til the nigga does something crazy?" Tray looked even more upset than me.

"Just forget it," I snapped.

He didn't respond since he saw my frustration.

Becky called on the Bluetooth on our way back and I explained to her what happened. "Mia, I know you're upset about this situation. How about I come over and take the kids for a couple days? Just to give you guys some breathing room to figure this out."

For the first time that day, I felt some sense of relief.

"How would you do that, though? What about your salon?"

"Girl, I'm not worried about my business. I have a full set of stylists who are just as capable of running things as me. I need a few days, anyway."

"Thank you so much, Becky."

Tray jumped in. "Yeah, good looking out, Beck."

Becky took the boys for three whole days, and tried to keep them for a fourth. Tray and I spent those three days making love, binge-watching shows, and getting much needed rest. I didn't want to let Becky keep them for the fourth day, but Tray said we should.

"It will give us some more time to bond," he said.

I smirked. "Ya nasty," I said.

"So are you."

I called Becky again just to make sure she was really offering to keep the boys another night, and not just saying it to be nice.

"Girl, ain't you tired?" I joked. "I know you're not used to waking up all hours of the day and night."

Becky chuckled. "No worries, Mia. I was built for this."

That brought a tear to my eye. If I didn't have a friend like Becky, I didn't know how I would have gotten through half of what I'd been going through.

Chapter 27: Mia

Becky and I decided to chill together for a few when she brought the boys back. Tray was at work, so it was just us two with the twins. My mom was out on another mysterious date with her new man.

She was all smiles when she told me about the first date, so I was happy for her.

"Girl, I cannot even explain to you how pissed I am at Noland," I said to Becky. "I sincerely can't stand his ass."

"Mm hm."

"I mean, what right does he have to think he can just waltz up in here and try to take my baby? After I was the one who laid there and pushed him out. How dare he?"

"Yup."

Becky was going silent on me for some reason.

"What's up?"

She sighed. "I've been listening to you rant about Noland for the past hour or so, Mia, but have you ever stopped to consider his side?"

I picked up my jaw from the floor. "His side? What do you mean?"

"I mean, he is Tyriek's father. He thought he had a whole future with you. He planned with you, proposed to you, tried to help you get over Tray... and then you still left him for your ex, and are raising his son with him."

"Becky, you know how crazy Noland was acting. Why are you saying all this now?"

She was silent for a moment. "Just because someone loves hard doesn't make them crazy. Besides, you should be grateful that even if he does get custody, you still will have at least one child in the house. Some of us can't have any."

She turned away after saying that.

Wow, I never knew. "You can't have kids?"

She shook her head. "I had an emergency surgery when I was sixteen. The doctors had to remove my uterus. When they told me I would never have children, I broke down. I would give anything to hear little feet running back and forth, or have somebody wake me up at three o'clock in the morning screaming at the top of their lungs. You should count yourself blessed."

It was my turn to be silent now.

"I'm so sorry to hear that, Becky."

"Yup." She was solemn for another moment, then her expression brightened. "But you know what though? I try not to dwell on that. I'm living my dreams right now, thanks to you, girl." She smiled at me and I gave her a halfhearted smile back. She took a serious tone again. "For real, Mia. I appreciate the fact that you pushed me out there, and guess what? I meant to tell you this earlier, but I have a bundles convention coming up next week. I might need a ride to the airport. Do you think you can bring me?" She looked like she felt bad for making me feel bad.

"Of course, girl. You know I gotchu."

Just then, there was a knock on the door.

I sucked my teeth. "Oh God, who is this?" The last time someone showed up unannounced, I was served papers to meet Noland's stupid ass in court.

I opened the door, and of course he was standing there with two police officers.

179

"Excuse me, Ma'am. Are you Mia Bradley?"

"Yes, I am." I glared at Noland.

"We're here for a wellness check, and your fiancé says that you haven't allowed him to see his son?"

I couldn't believe this nigga. "Former fiancé, and I'm fine. His son is also fine. Noland, why are you coming to my house with the police?"

He glared right back at me. "When you didn't answer your phone for a few days, I didn't know if something was wrong."

I sucked my teeth. "Oh, please. You know exactly why I was ignoring you. You need to stop all this bullshit."

"Please don't curse in front of my child."

I was so mad I wanted to punch him in the face. Obviously, I couldn't do that with the police right there.

The officer cut in. "Ma'am, do you mind if we see the child just to ensure that he is okay?"

I sighed and went over to the bassinets. Becky was already holding Tyrell, who apparently had just woken up, so I grabbed Tyriek, carrying him to the front door.

"Here he is. He's clean, he's fed, and he's safe."

"Can I hold my son, please?"

Noland had five more seconds to stand at my door before I cussed his ass clean out.

The officer stepped in again. "Ma'am, just for a few moments. We're right here."

I begrudgingly handed Tyriek to Noland. He made a big show of being extra careful with him like he was trying to protect him from me or something.

"Has he eaten yet?"

"He was just about to," I snapped. "Before you knocked on my door, causing drama."

The officer cut back in. "Okay, we'll leave you to feed your son then. Noland, please return the child to his mother."

Noland didn't move. "Why don't you let me take him for a day?"

"Hell no! After this stunt you pulled? You can see me in court since you like to play dirty."

Noland left with the police, and I took Tyriek back inside to feed him.

I really could not stand his ass. If he thought he was about to take my child from me, he was about to learn a serious lesson.

Tray

I swear, I wanted to bury this nigga.

When Mia told me how Noland came to the house with the cops, that was the last straw for me. Filing for full custody? Extreme, but that could just be seen as pettiness, but coming to the house with cops like Mia was crazy or something? That was below the belt. The worst part about this was that there was nothing I could do to change it.

The best I could do was be there for my woman as she fought against this man.

It wasn't like she was holding his son from him or anything. We literally let Becky watch the boys for four days. The nigga was such a control freak, it was crazy.

I looked over at Mia on the couch. The expression on her face told me she was deep in thought, probably about Noland.

Then her phone buzzed with a notification.

She swiped her screen to check it, then sucked her teeth. "See, this is too much, but now I'm almost sure it's Noland behind this."

I perked up at that. "Noland is behind what?"

She looked at me. "I think Noland was the one who pushed me in front of the car that day, as well as the person who almost ran me over a while ago, and I think he's the one sending me all these emails." She got up from her seat on the couch and walked over to the loveseat where I was. She showed me her screen.

This will all be over soon, bitch. Hope you know how to duck.

I looked at the address it was sent from, and it was a random combination of letters and numbers from an unrecognizable domain name.

"You say you have more like this?"

She nodded. "I've gotten a few of them over the past year."

"How come you didn't tell the cops about this?"

"I wasn't sure who it was. I had multiple people I knew who could have done it. Loryn, Evelin from my job, and Noland, but Noland is the common factor in all this."

"You started getting all these messages once you met him?"

She shook her head. "No, it started before I met him, but he's the only logical person I can think of. I mean, look at what he's doing now."

She had a good point, but I still wasn't sure it was him.

"I actually got some random text messages myself from a private number."

Her eyes widened. "Show me!"

I sighed. "I didn't save them. Sorry. I thought it was somebody playing on the phone. I never had anything threatening happen to me, so I left it alone. Besides, it was a private number, anyway."

"Damn."

We stared at each other for a second.

Mia spoke again. "If we can find a way to trace these emails back to Noland, that should be enough for a restraining order, and for him to lose the custody battle."

I agreed. "I'm all in. Let's see if we can figure this out."

Chapter 28: Mia

Noland was dead set on showing his ass.

We went to court, and of course the judge was basically saying that she wasn't about to grant him full custody since there was no reason to.

Then Noland had the nerve to say he had video evidence of sexual abuse.

"Sexual abuse?" I said, but the judge quieted me.

"Have you contacted Child Protective Services about these allegations, Mr. Rogers?"

Noland looked uneasy. "No, your honor, but she and her fiancé were having sex right in front of my son. That's completely inappropriate."

"What's inappropriate is you having cameras in my house without my permission!" I wanted to jump across that aisle and swing on him so bad.

Tray was also fuming next to me.

The judge brought order back to the room. "Mr. Rogers, I see no evidence for us to grant you full custody. You can file for joint custody, but Ms. Bradley appears more than capable of caring for Tyriek."

"Your honor, they are placing my child in an unsafe environment. She lets her friends come and take him whenever they please. That opens him up to all kinds of things that I can't protect him from."

The judge looked like she was done with Noland. "Mr. Rogers, you are going to have to have a conversation with Ms. Bradley about who the child is allowed around. That is not something handled by the courts unless it becomes a legal matter. Case dismissed."

Thank God.

I didn't even look at his ass on the way out, but I heard his voice loud and clear as Tray and I made our way to the parking lot.

"This isn't over, Mia. It's only just begun."

I tensed, but Tray was already on it. "Eyo, nigga. Move around. You already lost, and you know damn well you was bullshitting in that courtroom. You just mad the judge saw right through you."

Noland didn't bother responding to Tray, probably since Tray wasn't Noland's target, anyway.

When we got home, I kicked off my shoes and flopped on the couch, feeling exhausted already and it wasn't even noon yet. Then I had to jump up again when Becky called. I forgot I was supposed to bring her to the airport. I went and saw my friend off, wishing her well at the bundles convention, then went back home to my stressful and depressing life. Tray's mom was watching the boys while we were at court, and she was supposed to be bringing them back in a couple of hours, but when Tray saw the look on my face, he immediately called and asked her to keep them overnight.

Thankfully, she agreed.

"Tray, I don't want my baby around Noland," I said when he got off the phone with his mom. "I really don't think he's stable."

Tray was silent for a second. "I don't think he would try to hurt him, though. He's just pissed you broke up with him. It's clear he was really feeling you."

That stung, because I knew he really did care for me, but fuck Noland. I understood that he was mad I chose

Tray, but to try to take my baby away for it, and spread my name through the courts?

That shit was uncalled for.

"I want to hire a private investigator," I announced. "Have somebody spy on his ass for once."

"What is that gonna solve, Mia?"

"I don't know and I don't care. He thinks he can do whatever he wants to do with my privacy. Two can play that game."

Chapter 29: Mia

This nightmare just kept getting worse and worse. Tyriek was gone.

Tray went out to chill with his boys, Ant and Trev, and to get a little break for an hour or two. The twins were up to four-hour naps, so I figured we were cool.

I was groggy myself, so I brought them into their nursery. I set my alarm for three hours just to make sure I had ample time to get up for their feeding, but when I woke up on schedule, I went to their cribs and noticed that Tyrell was there, but Tyriek wasn't.

My mind immediately grew frantic. "Tyriek!" I yelled, as if he could answer me. I practically tore that room apart trying to convince myself that somehow he had gained enough strength in his limbs to climb out of his crib in the span of three hours.

Once I allowed it to hit me what happened, I called Tray's phone.

He barely got a chance to say hello before I was screaming in his ear. "Noland stole my baby!"

"What?" he asked like he couldn't believe his ears.

"Noland took Tyriek, Tray."

"I'm on my way."

Tray hung up the phone, and I was a nervous wreck.

My mind went to calling the police, but I decided to wait until Tray got home. I checked, rechecked, and checked again to make sure that Tyrell was okay. Surprisingly, he hadn't awakened during all my carrying on.

I dialed Noland's number, but his phone went straight to voicemail.

"That motherfucker! I'm gonna kill him!" All I saw was red. I thought the court date was the last straw, but Noland was about to make me catch a case. Then I went to feeling guilty. I should have changed the locks again after Noland left. If his crazy ass was capable of setting up cameras without my consent, he was also liable to waltz in and do something like this. I was consumed by guilt, then my emotions switched back to rage.

How dare he come into my house and take my baby while I was asleep?

He was that mad the judge wouldn't let him take Tyriek away from me?

I was gonna kill him. Noland was dead.

I paced back and forth, trying to develop a plan while calling Noland three more times. Each time, his phone went straight to voicemail.

I felt like my mind was breaking from reality. Everything inside me was beginning to snap.

Tray arrived less than twenty minutes later. "What happened?" he asked, looking just as frantic as I felt on the inside.

"I went to take a nap, and I woke up and Tyriek was gone."

Tray stared at me for a few seconds, then balled his fists. "We gotta call the cops."

"Fuck the cops. I wanna go over there, guns blazing!"

Tray was already on the phone. "Hello? I would like to report a kidnapping..."

We arrived at Noland's house the same time the cops got there. Noland's car wasn't outside. My heart dropped when I realized that. My baby could be anywhere with him.

Then, as if it was by a stroke of miracle, Noland pulled up the street and into his driveway like it was nothing.

He had passed right by the cops like he couldn't see them stationed there on his street.

When he got out, however, two officers approached him. "Noland Rogers?" one of them asked.

He looked like he was confused. "Yes?"

I was trembling internally as I watched their interaction. Tray and I were standing by his car, and he was holding me.

The cops asked him about Tyriek's whereabouts.

That was when Noland noticed us standing there. "Tyriek's whereabouts? What the hell is going on, Mia?"

My heart dropped as I understood what was going on. It wasn't him. Noland became just as frantic as I was when I looked into Tyriek's crib and noticed him missing.

"Are you telling me my son was kidnapped?" Noland's voice had risen a few octaves. He took a step toward me, but the officer held his hand up to tell him not to move further. "Where the fuck is my son, Mia?"

"Somebody took him," I said.

"What do you mean, somebody took him? You can't be telling me this. See, this is why I took your ass to court. You wouldn't let me see my son, and now you done fucked around and let somebody take him."

Even though that wasn't how it happened, Noland's words still struck me like a dart. I saw the pain, confusion, and frustration in his features.

The officer turned back to me.

"Do you have any idea where he could be?"

Tray and I went through hours of questioning at the police station, trying to figure out what could have happened to Tyriek.

My mom was watching Tyrell for us while we tried to handle this.

While we were with the officers, Tray was adamant that Noland had something to do with it, but I was no longer convinced of that. I saw the look in his eyes. Plus, Noland had shown them proof that he was at work doing a double shift when the incident happened. His time sheet and camera footage from his job showed that. I suggested Loryn, since Tray said that she had been doing crazy shit like popping up at his job and keying his car, but Tray said that wouldn't make sense since she barely took care of Briella. He couldn't see her taking Tyriek on top of that.

We were back to square one. My baby could be anywhere.

As we were leaving the station, Tray kept on it. "Noland could have hired somebody, Mia. Niggas lie everyday..."

He stopped when I held my hand up. I understood he was just trying to help, but I didn't want speculation. I wanted my baby back.

On the way home, I snapped and told Tray to bring me to Loryn's house.

"Mia, she didn't..."

"You think she didn't, just like I don't think Noland did it. Go there, now."

He obeyed, and when we got there, I was out of the car before he could put the gear in Park. I banged on Loryn's front door like I was the police.

"Mia, calm down," Tray said, coming to stand with me as we waited.

Loryn answered the door looking frazzled. She was wearing a bonnet and wiping sleep out of her eyes, but when she saw Tray, she froze.

Her eyes filled with hope. "You're coming back?" she asked him.

I cut in. "Where the fuck is my baby, bitch!"

She sucked her teeth like she just noticed I was there. "How the hell should I know?"

I pushed past her to walk into her house, but she swung on me. We got into it, but Tray used all of his strength to pull us apart.

"Come on, come on!" he said. "We didn't come here for that!"

Loryn was holding her busted lip. "Bitch, I said I don't have your kid!"

I wasn't hearing her. "Where is he?"

I was so mad, I was flipping couch cushions, upending drawers, and then I felt bad when I went to Loryn's bedroom and saw that I had awakened her baby, Briella. She was screaming at the top of her lungs.

Tyriek wasn't here, and I had just scared that baby for no reason.

I walked back to Loryn's living room filled with frustration and guilt. Loryn couldn't do anything to stop me while I was ransacking her apartment because Tray had been holding her back when she tried to go after me.

He let her go so she could tend to her child.

She roughly bumped me out of the way as she was passing me to get to her room, but I didn't respond. I felt so defeated.

"Tray, where is he?" I croaked.

His expression was pained. "I don't know, baby."

We exited Loryn's apartment and she held Briella in one arm while slamming the door with her opposite hand.

Tray and I drove home. I felt so lost and confused.

I spent hours sitting at the kitchen table with Tray, agonizing about Tyriek. Where was my baby?

I got a call from a private number at midnight that answered my question. I had bought a bottle of Henny to try to clear my mind. It wasn't doing anything for me.

When the number called, at first, I wasn't going to answer, but when I considered the time of night and the fact that it was private, I gave in.

"Hello?"

"You lucky, bitch," she spat.

I sat alert. "Who is this?"

"Oh, you forgot my voice that quick?"

What the fuck...? "Becky?"

She snorted. "That's right, bitch!"

"What the hell is going on?" My mind was swimming.

Becky sighed. "Mia, you were never one for common sense. I bet you been wondering about where Tyriek is."

I almost knocked over the bottle of Henny, trying to get Tray's attention. He was high out of his mind.

He turned to me.

"Becky has Tyriek!" I hissed.

He blinked at me. "What? Why?"

Becky answered as I put her on speaker. "It's all your fault, Mia. You put the boys in the wrong cribs."

"Becky, what are you talking about?" I asked. "Where is my baby?"

"He's my baby now, bitch! Unless you make this right."

"Make it right how?"

She continued as if I hadn't spoken. "I ended up taking Tyriek's funky ass instead of Tyrell. Tyrell is my son, not Tyriek."

"Both of the boys are my sons, Becky!"

"No! Tyrell is mine! I'll kill you!"

Something was seriously wrong with her. "Becky, where are you?" I tried to calm myself down to see if I could reason with her.

She laughed. "Don't think you are gonna catch me with the okey doke. You're the dumb one, not me."

"Why did you take my baby?"

Her tone became filled with impatience like she was explaining something to someone for the umpteenth time. "First of all, Tyrell is my son. I mistakenly took Tyriek, so I will be glad to give him back to you. Bring my baby to the docks on Friday at noon, or I'm throwing Tyriek in the river. Any sign of cops, and he's dead. Do we understand each other?"

Friday was two days from today. "Becky, why are you doing this?"

She hung up.

I never felt so desperate, lost, and confused in my life. I thought Becky was my friend. Why would she? How could she...?

As if she heard my thoughts, Becky called from the private number again.

"You know what?" she said like she was in the middle of an argument with me. "You know what? I'm-a tell you why. It's because you're selfish, entitled ass always got what you wanted, while me and Loryn were struggling for leftovers."

I wasn't following her. "Are you telling me Loryn is in on this?"

Becky laughed, and she was sounding more maniacal by the second. "No, that bitch had bricks for brains. What she tried to do with Tray was cute, but I had my eyes on him first. Her plan would never work, but mine will."

I looked at Tray, who appeared to be just as confused as me. Becky continued.

"Okay, let me spell it out for your stupid ass since you never could put two and two together. Remember the day you met my man?"

"What man?"

"Tray, idiot!" I heard her snapping her fingers on the other end. Then I heard a baby's cry in the background. My heart immediately went to Tyriek. My son was over there with this psychopath and wasn't shit I could do about it.

"Becky, please just bring back my son," I said as we heard him continue to whine.

Becky took on a flippant tone. "Oh, girl, hush. All I gotta do is rub a little more rum under his gums and he'll be back to sleep."

My nostrils flared. "You gave my baby alcohol?"

She continued her previous story, as if she hadn't heard me. "Anyway, where was I? Oh yeah, the day you stole my man from me. Bitch, I gave you a simple direction. You go over there, you get his attention, and you send him to me, but you didn't listen, did you? You had to take him for yourself like you did with everything!"

"Becky, what are you talking about? That's not even how that happened!"

"Like I said," Becky continued without missing a beat. "You took him from me, even though I told you I wanted him, so since I can't have Tray, I'll have the next best thing. If you don't bring Tyrell tomorrow, consider this your goodbye to Tyriek." The next thing I heard was my baby screaming in the background like Becky had put the phone up to his mouth, then the line went dead.

I turned to Tray. "We gotta go back to the cops."

Chapter 30: Mia

We went to the police, and they went to Becky's house as we followed, but her apartment was empty like she had moved out.

The entire ride over there I was wondering how this could have happened right under my nose. The emails, the text messages... How could it have been Becky? Was she working with someone else? Was Loryn really in on it, and Becky was lying? I didn't know what to think.

Neither me nor Tray slept that night.

The police tried to trace Becky's phone, but her old phone was the only thing she left in her apartment. It was sitting there on the kitchen counter like she had been waiting for this moment to make me out to be the biggest fool of the century.

It didn't make sense, though. I had dropped Becky off at the airport a couple of days ago! Then I remembered that I didn't actually meet her at her house to pick her up. We met at a store because she said she was running late and had to grab a few things. My stupid ass believed her, not realizing it was a coverup the entire time.

How could I know, though? Becky was always my rider. She defended me against Loryn and encouraged me to move on when Tray cheated.

I never saw this coming.

By the time nine o'clock hit, I was more frantic than I'd ever been. "Tray, take me to Becky's salon."

He looked like he was in a daze. "She's not there, Mia."

My eyes clouded. "I know, but maybe one of her employees will know what happened. Where she could be."

He didn't protest, though I knew he was thinking we were wasting our time, not to mention overstepping the police officers.

There was an Amber Alert out on my baby. This could not be life.

I had gotten all types of calls from old friends, messages, everything. I appreciated the fact that people were concerned, but I didn't want their concern. I wanted Tyriek.

When we got to the salon, the only person there was Bria.

"Bria?" I said, my nose wrinkling when I entered the building. "What are you doing here?" Bria was the stylist at Monica's salon that Becky said cost her her job.

Bria looked at me like I was crazy. "What do you mean, what am I doing here?"

I tried to put two and two together. "Did you and Becky reconcile?"

Bria stared at me. "Reconcile... Mia, what are you talking about?"

I tried again. "Becky told me you two didn't like each other and that there was a big blow-up at Monica's salon. That's why she started this business."

Bria chuckled as if I just told a joke. "Wow, that's what she told you? Yeah, Monica was a bitch, but me and Becky never had a problem with each other. We were always cool. When she got fired, I felt bad. I was sick of Monica's ass, anyway, so I told her we should go into business together."

I picked my jaw up from the floor as Bria continued.

"Becky's credit wasn't good enough to get this salon in her name, plus she didn't have enough money saved to put a big enough down payment for them to accept her, so I took over. I liked the business side more than anything, so I told Becky she could be the face of the salon while I handled all the behind-the-scenes stuff."

All of this was confusing me. "So, Becky is not the owner." I said that more like a statement than a question, but Bria apparently understood.

She pursed her lips. "Nope. I am. Becky was my star stylist until she waltzed in here a week ago and said she was moving out of state."

My heart dropped as I took a step closer. "Did she tell you where she was going?"

Bria shook her head. "No. I actually don't spend a lot of time here in the salon. I had only come that day because I had to replenish some of our products. Becky's announcement shocked the hell out of me. I thought she was happy here."

My mind was swimming. "She didn't tell you anything about where she was going?"

Bria shook her head again. "Like I said, I was just as surprised as you appear to be. Aren't you her best friend, though? What's going on with y'all?"

I wasn't sure if I should trust Bria with this information, especially since she looked like she was just trying to get the tea on me and Becky's relationship, anyway, but I was desperate for answers. Maybe Bria was holding back.

"Becky stole my baby. We put out an Amber Alert, and I'm working with the police to try to figure out where she might have gone."

Tray grabbed my arm as I was speaking as if to tell me to slow down with how much I told her, but I didn't believe Bria was in on this.

Not that I should trust my judgement, anyway, since apparently I was horrible at discerning people's motives.

Bria clapped her hand over her mouth. "What?" Her eyes widened. "I just heard about that on the news this morning on my way here. That was your baby? Oh my God, Mia. Are you okay?" She reached out to touch me.

She's sincere, my mind told me. "No, I'm not okay, Bria. I need to find out where Becky is before she does something terrible."

We left Bria just as some officers were showing up to ask her the same questions I just asked. Slow asses. I prayed they would find something I hadn't found, however.

"You think we should call Noland?" Tray asked when we got in the car.

Just then, Tray's phone rang. The detectives had my phone because they were trying to trace the private number Becky had called me from.

"Hello?" he answered. "Okay, yeah, we'll be there." He hung up.

"Who was that?" I asked.

"The detectives. They said they want us to come to the station."

When we got there, my mind was going haywire. I prayed that whatever they had to tell us was good news.

Noland surprised us both by arriving at the same time we did.

"What are you doing here?" I asked.

"What the hell do you mean, what am I doing here?" he asked. Noland looked just as crazy as I felt. I could tell he hadn't slept since he heard the news, either. I felt bad for not calling him immediately to tell him about Becky, but I didn't say anything. We entered the station together.

Detective Stanley greeted us. "Good, you're all here." He gave us a thin-lipped smile, then led us to a private room.

"Are there any updates?" Noland asked as soon as we sat down.

It was then that I noticed Detective Stanley was holding my phone. He held it out to me, and I took it.

Detective Stanley cleared his throat. "We were able to trace the private number to a prepaid phone that was purchased the next town over."

Noland cut in. "What private number?" He looked back and forth between us and the detective.

I swallowed. "My friend Becky has Tyriek."

"Becky? How do you know?" Noland was pissed I hadn't told him, I could tell.

"She called us last night." I looked at Detective Stanley, then back at Noland. "She told us she meant to take Tyrell rather than Tyriek, and said we had to meet her by the docks tomorrow at noon or she was going to throw Tyriek in the river."

"That bitch ain't killing my baby!" Noland thundered, banging his fist on the table.

Detective Stanley tried to calm him. "Listen, Noland, we're all upset about this news, but I'll have you know that we are doing everything possible to get your son back safe."

"Clearly y'all ain't doing enough! Why am I just being told about this?"

Detective Stanley looked embarrassed, and I felt bad. He probably thought I had been keeping Noland informed, seeing as he was the father.

"I'm sorry about that. It won't happen again." He turned to me and Tray. "One thing I do have to say is, please don't interfere with our investigation again. My partner alerted me to the fact that you had already gone to the salon where Becky worked before we got there. We have officers trained on asking the right questions, and you going there could tamper with evidence."

"I was just trying to find my son..." I started, but he held his hand up.

"I understand that, but please don't interfere again." He looked at Noland. "Understood?"

"Yup," Noland said, but he looked like the idea of not interfering was the last thing on his mind.

Noland didn't say a word to us as we all exited the station together, then he peeled out of the parking lot.

Tray and I were exhausted, but when we went home, we couldn't get any rest due to worrying about Tyriek.

Hours went by, before the detectives called us again and told us that their new plan was to try to get to the docks without Becky knowing they were there. We were going to meet with her, as she said, but they would intercept the arrangement and arrest her.

I didn't think that was a good idea, but Detective Stanley said that was the best they could do.

When would this nightmare end?

Tray

Mia was all over the place, and so was I. Our son was out there with a crazy woman and there was nothing we could do about it. Tyriek was Noland's biologically, but I loved him the same as I did Tyrell.

I wished this was like the movies where we could get a magical clue to tell us where Becky was, then track her down and get Tyriek back. This wasn't a movie though, unfortunately, and Tyriek was in very real danger.

We decided to go to Becky's mom's house when Mia grew too antsy to just keep waiting to hear more from the detectives. I tried to calm her, but she was adamant on finding answers. I couldn't blame her.

Becky's mom revealed to us that Becky had been diagnosed with a delusional disorder during her teens. Becky told her she'd stopped taking her meds recently because she figured she could handle it.

Mia was floored when she heard that, and so was I. Neither of us had ever heard that about her. Becky's mom, Shyanne, said she thought Mia knew.

"Girl, Becky told me she informed you of her disorder years ago!" Shyanne said. "She said you went to a few of her therapy sessions and everything."

Apparently, Becky was a hell of a liar on top of her disorder.

Mia begged Shyanne not to tell the cops we had been by there, and Shyanne agreed. "Girl, I know how it is. As wild as Becky's imagination was as a child, if something happened to her, I would be out there just like you. Your secret is safe with me."

Shyanne sounded very encouraging, but part of me didn't trust her. If she knew her daughter was delusional, it was possible Becky told her she thought Mia's baby was hers. If she did, why didn't her mom say anything? That was dangerous shit, and it led to where we were now.

My mind also went to the idea that Shyanne's mother was possibly in on Tyriek's disappearance. I didn't tell Mia any of my suspicions, though because she was already distraught. I wanted to alleviate her pain and confusion as much as I could.

On the way back home, Noland called Mia's phone and she put him on speaker.

He was furious. "Why the hell didn't y'all tell me that Becky had Tyriek?"

Mia tried to apologize for not letting him know sooner about Becky, but he cut her off.

"Naw, fuck y'all!" he said. "Y'all been acting this whole time like it's not my DNA running through that baby. I can't believe this shit."

I understood him. As a man, if somebody I loved was in danger, I would want to know every detail. Nobody could deny that Noland loved Tyriek.

Noland trusted us to keep him informed, and we dropped the ball.

When we got home, Mia turned to me on the couch. Her eyes clouded. "What are we supposed to do, Tray? Just sit here? She could be out there doing anything to my baby. This is all my fucking fault!"

She broke all the way down, collapsing into herself.

I immediately reached for her and wrapped her up in my arms. "Baby, it's gonna be okay. We gonna find him, okay?"

When I said that, she let out a sound I had never heard before, and never wanted to hear again. It was a wail from the depths of her soul.

I wasn't a religious man, but I found myself reaching back to when my mom used to pray during my childhood. "Lord Jesus," I said. "God, please help Tyriek come back to us safe. Please."

My own vision blurred, and me and Mia's bodies blended into each other. We literally clung to each other and to God for dear life in that moment.

Chapter 31: Mia

Another sleepless night. I'd already started hallucinating. I would doze off for a few seconds, then wake up and it was like I could see Tyriek hovering over me, reaching out for me. He couldn't talk yet, of course, but in my hallucinations he would say, "Mommy!" and his little fingers would desperately grasp for mine. I would go at him full force, but no matter how close I got, he was still out of my reach.

Tray tried to help me manage. "Mia, we're gonna find him."

"You don't know that, Tray." I tried not to think the worst, but I was thinking it. Who knew how far Becky's delusion would go? What if her mind told her that Tyriek was now her enemy or something? What if she did something to him despite us meeting her at the docks?

Twelve o'clock could not come fast enough. Detective Stanley came to our house at five o'clock in the morning to go over the plan. "Here's what we're going to do," he said.

Before he could open his mouth to say anything else, he got a call. "Stanley," he answered.

Then his eyes bulged. "What?" His face reddened, and my heart dropped. *No!* My mind screamed. I prayed this was not about my baby. I grabbed Tray's hand and braced myself. If something happened to my baby, I didn't know what I was going to do.

Stanley's face was getting redder by the second. He looked completely pissed off at whoever was on the other line. "Yes, bring them here," he said.

Then he hung up and faced us after taking a deep breath.

"I have good news," he said.

I blinked. If it was such good news, why was he so pissed?

I opened my mouth to ask what the news was, but he continued. "Apparently, you guys taking matters into your own hands has paid off. Noland found Tyriek."

My heart lurched. "Found Tryiek? Where? Where is my baby?"

Now I had both of my hands clutching Detective Stanley's forearms and I was screeching my words in his face, but he seemed to understand. He'd calmed from his anger and spoke in a soothing voice.

"Hey. It's okay. Your son is safe. I have some officers escorting Noland and Tyriek here now. You'll be reunited soon."

He was right.

A cruiser pulled up less than ten minutes later with Noland and Tyriek in the back seat. Noland was holding him in his arms.

I was over by the passenger side door before anyone said a word.

When Noland stepped out, however, he wasn't trying to let me get my son.

He snatched away from me as I reached for Tyriek. "No!" he said, his voice forceful. "It's your fault this happened, Mia. If I hadn't remembered I put a tracking device on Becky's car, my son would be dead!"

"Tracking device?" Tray asked.

Noland's eyes shifted. "Yeah, I had one on Mia's car, and Becky's in case she and Mia got in an accident, and yours."

"Mine?" Tray said.

Noland's face showed no remorse. "I had to know if you were fucking my girl, man."

Noland's ass was crazy as hell, but I guessed in a severely misguided way, he got something right this time. My son was safe.

"Noland. Please. You know I love him just as much as you," I urged. The hardness of his expression softened, but only slightly.

He held Tyriek out, and I grabbed him. I was in shock. I inspected every inch of his body as Detective Stanley, Tray, and Noland watched.

"We're going to have to take him to the hospital, Mia," Detective Stanley said. "I only had the officers bring Noland and Tyriek here first because they were so close by."

"Of course," I replied, turning back to him.

Noland cut in. "But after the hospital, he needs to come home with me."

I froze. I wasn't trying to do this today, but Noland needed to watch it.

Detective Stanley clapped back at Noland. "No, after the hospital, all of you need to come to the station. We have to discuss what happened and how you found the baby."

Noland looked at Detective Stanley like he was crazy. "What do you mean, you need to know how I found the baby? I told y'all. I had a tracking device on Becky's car. I tracked it and that's how I found her."

Detective Stanley stood firm. "We still need to go over the details to close out the case."

Things went back and forth between tension and elation after that. Tray, Noland, and I went to the hospital to have Tyriek checked out. Thankfully, he was fine despite the fact that Becky told me she put rum on his gums to make him sleep.

The doctors said there didn't appear to be any issues with him that they could see.

As for Becky, Noland had brought handcuffs with him, along with a gun, to get Tyriek back from her. He caught up with her at a gas station. Apparently, she had been hiding out in a cheap motel, paying cash only.

She left Tyriek in the car by himself while she went in the store, and when she came out, Noland sprang up on her, scaring her with his gun and demanding she give him the keys to the car.

She gave him the keys, and he subdued and cuffed her, got Tyriek out of her car, and called the police.

Detective Stanley was furious to hear these details. "Listen, Noland. I understand you wanted your son back, but you interfered with a police investigation in the process of doing this. You should have told us about the tracking device you had on Becky's car. I'm not going to charge you, but please, never interfere with a police investigation again."

"Yup," Noland replied, but everyone in the room knew he would do it again in a heartbeat. I couldn't blame him because I was the same way.

When we were leaving the station, escorted by Detective Stanley, however, Noland tried again to take Tyriek. "It's only right, Mia."

I tried my best to remain calm. "Noland, we can discuss a better arrangement tomorrow, but Tyriek is staying with me tonight."

"You got him kidnapped, though."

I felt myself growing hot, and Detective Stanley must have sensed it. He stepped in. "Listen, who has custody?"

"I do," I said.

"Okay, so Noland, you're going to have to let Mia take Tyriek tonight. I trust that she will let you see your son in the morning."

Noland had tears in his eyes. "That's what I get for saving his life? A slap on the wrist like I committed a crime, and my son taken away yet again?"

Tray interjected. "It's not like that, man."

"Fuck you, nigga!" Noland thundered. "The only reason I don't bust your ass right now is because I know these cops will lock me up."

Tray was heated, I could tell. "Look, Noland. I been patient with you because I understand where you're coming from, but you're not going to continually disrespect me or my woman. I'm only going to say this one time. You don't want these problems."

Noland backed down, but only slightly. "Your woman? Yeah... y'all ain't seen a problem yet. I'll be filing for a new custody case ASAP."

The saga was going to continue, I guessed.

And it did. We spent the whole rest of the day hugging and holding Tyriek, but the next morning, after we finally had a good night's sleep with Tyriek lying between me and Tray in bed, I was awakened by police knocking on my door.

"What is it now?" I asked. I had brought a sleeping Tyriek to the door with me. Tray being there or not, I was never letting him out of my sight again.

Detective Stanley's face held its customary grim expression. "Mia, I'm going to need you and Tray to come to the station."

"For what?" Tray asked. He had just appeared by my side.

"I think you both already know."

"What are you talking about?" I asked.

He sighed like he was ready to be done with our asses. "Noland's car was run off the road last night by a mysterious vehicle. He's in the hospital fighting for his life. We need you to come in for questioning."

Chapter 32: Mia

This nightmare was literally never going to end. After all the drama we went through getting Tyriek back from Becky and having her locked up, now we had to turn around and have Tray's mom watch Tyriek since my mom was watching Tyrell already. Tray said we should just leave both boys with my mom, but this whole situation had me paranoid and confused as hell. It made sense to me to have each boy watched by one of our mothers so they could both have someone's full attention.

Tray and I went to the station, and of course, they took us to separate rooms.

"This has to be a joke," I said when Detective Stanley came into my room.

He studied me before speaking. "Mia, you have to know that it's a strange coincidence for you, Tray, and Noland to have a huge blowup like the one you did in front of me yesterday, then all of a sudden, supposedly some random stranger runs him off the road later that night?"

I couldn't believe he was accusing me like this. I decided to set him straight. "Look, Detective. I am a mother and I was fighting for my son. What happened to Noland is unfortunate, but I had nothing to do with it."

He wasn't convinced, I could tell. "So that's it? No care or concern for a man you were previously engaged to? A man who fathered one of your children?"

He was getting to me. Of course, I was innocent, but Detective Stanley was making me sound like a heartless bitch.

"I do feel bad, but..."

He cut me off. "So why haven't you asked how he was doing?"

I felt stupid as hell, but I asked anyway. "How is he?"

He sighed like he had me right where he wanted me. "Not good at all, Mia. The doctors are sustaining him for now, but they say there's a chance that he might not make it through the night."

That caused my heart to drop. When they mentioned the accident before, I was shocked, but to hear that Noland might die was a different story.

"Are you serious?"

Detective Stanley nodded. "Yes, I'm serious. Do you have any idea who might have done this?"

I tried to wrack my brains. "The only person I could have thought of would have been Becky since she's the one who took Tyriek, but you guys still have her in custody, right? She didn't break out, I assume."

Detective Stanley shot me a thin-lipped smile. "No, she didn't. Our department is competent enough to do our jobs, for your information."

That was what this was about. He was still pissed at me, Tray, and Noland overstepping his investigation. I tried to redirect.

"Look, like I said, I'm sorry this happened to Noland, but this whole situation is a nightmare I want to end, not continue. I had nothing to do with Noland's accident."

"Mm hm." Detective Stanley clicked his pen like he still didn't believe me. "What about your fiancé, Tray? He must have been pretty upset after that argument, too. It looks like he and Noland were about to come to blows."

"Tray slept in the bed right next to me last night."

"Hm. Are you sure he slept the whole night?"

"What are you implying?"

He repositioned himself in his seat. "Is it possible that Tray could have slipped out while you and Tyriek were asleep?"

"No! What reason would he have to do that? Noland was not a threat to us. He already lost one custody case. All he was going to do was lose this one, too."

"Maybe Tray wasn't so convinced. After all, the child was kidnapped under your care."

That was a low blow, and he knew it. "Fuck you!" I screamed. "I'm leaving this place now, unless you feel like you have evidence to arrest me. Otherwise, you can talk to my lawyer."

I didn't even have a lawyer, but Detective Stanley had no idea how his words made me feel.

I stepped out of the room, then immediately felt awkward because Tray was still being questioned in another room. I prayed his story lined up with mine and that they didn't find cause to arrest him.

They couldn't, right?

All of this was making me feel like I was about to snap. I just wanted to say forget it all and move to Bermuda or something.

I did hope Noland was okay, though. Crazy or not, he did get my son back.

Chapter 33: Mia

Tense wasn't the word. When Tray came out of his interrogation room, he didn't look any better than I felt.

We were mostly silent on the way home.

When we pulled up, I finally turned to him. "Do you think we should hire a lawyer?"

Tray nodded. "They really want to get us for this, Mia. You should have seen the way that lady cop was threatening me."

"Detective Stanley was no better. He basically talked to me like I was guilty. Then he suggested that you went out and did it while I was asleep."

Tray shook his head. "The lady cop did the same thing to me."

I could not believe we were going through this. I wished we could go back to that night we had the argument that unknowingly at the time served as a catalyst for all this...

That night, me and Tray were mad at each other because ironically, I'd accused him of cheating.

There was a person named Sam in his phone that had called him a few times while he was at the gym. He had accidentally left his phone at home, so when Sam called the fourth time, I answered.

"Hello?"

A woman's voice came through the line. "Hello, may I speak to Tray?"

I wrinkled my nose. "And who are you?"

The bitch came back at me with attitude. "I'm his coworker."

"His coworker, huh?" I shot back. "And why is a coworker calling my man's phone?"

She chuckled. "Um, maybe because your man gave it to me."

"He gave it to you?" My ears were ringing, I was so heated.

She sounded like she loved getting under my skin. "Yes, honey. He sure did. All in the break room. Anyway, tell him to call me when he gets in."

CLICK.

The bitch had the audacity to hang up in my face.

Heated wasn't the word.

When Tray came home, I had something for his ass. I cursed him clean out before he fully got in the front door.

He acted like he was completely clueless as to why.

"You think you can have bitches calling your phone while you're living in my house? Huh, bitch nigga?" I screamed.

"Bitch nigga? What the fuck are you on, Mia?" He was clearly hurt by my words, but I kept going.

I crossed my arms. "Who the fuck is Sam, Tray."

He wrinkled his nose. "Sam? What the hell are you talking about?"

I whipped out his phone and showed him all the missed calls. "Yeah, you tried to change her name to a nigga's name, but she called you, dumbass."

He looked like he still wasn't putting two and two together. "Mia, I..." Before he could finish his sentence, Sam called again, and Tray answered.

"Who is this?" he asked, still playing dumb, or so I thought.

"What do you mean, Tray?" she said, and as soon as he heard her voice, Tray's expression changed.

"Oh, my fucking..." he sighed, then turned to me. "Mia, this is not what you think."

"Excuse me?" I heard Sam's loud ass on the other line.

He put her on speaker before he said his next words. "Listen, Sam. Whatever Trev said to you, he was just playing. I have a girlfriend. I'm sorry."

"What?" she said, her pompous attitude from before completely gone now. "What do you mean?"

"He gave you my number as a prank, Sam."

She was silent on the other line.

"Okay?" Tray said after a few moments, to make sure she heard him.

"Yup," she said in a hollow voice, then hung up.

Tray turned to me, suddenly re-pissed. "You really believed I would cheat on you?"

I was completely embarrassed, so I just said anything to save face. "You can play the game if you want to, Tray, but why was her number saved?"

"Mia, Trev did that. He was trying to get back at me for giving this older lady his number who was flirting with him."

I stepped back like I was appalled. "Oh, so that's what y'all do all day? Flirt with the ladies, huh?"

"Look, I'm about to get in the shower. We can talk more when I get out." He went toward the stairs.

"You do that," I called after him. "And make sure you hurry up, too because I'm gonna get in there next. Me and my girls are heading out tonight. Maybe I can find a nigga to flirt with."

He turned back. "Oh yeah? Well, me, Trev, and Ant haven't had a night out in a while, either."

216

And that was how it went. I ended up leaving before him just to be an asshole, dressed up completely like a slut, then I changed my mind halfway to Becky's house and went back home. When I got back home, Tray was already gone. He didn't come home until the next morning, so I screamed on him again, but then I felt bad about the argument and texted him all day. He was pissed at me, so he didn't respond. When he got home, I screamed on him again, then we had angry makeup sex after I apologized for jumping the gun.

Now here we were.

Tray looked up different lawyers while I cooked dinner. Both of us were starving, though this situation with Noland's accident was looming.

We ate our dinner mostly in silence, then headed to bed.

The next morning, Tray and I were preparing to go pick up the boys from our respective mother's houses when Detective Stanley called my phone.

"Hello, Mia? Is Tray with you?" he asked.

"Oh my God... what is it now? We already answered all of your questions!" I was not trying to do this today. Tray and I needed some semblance of sanity.

He stammered as he spoke. "It appears... We might have... Can you come to the station, please?"

I sighed and looked at Tray. "Okay, but we're not staying all day. We do have children to take care of, you know."

The whole drive to the station, we prayed that this wasn't more bad news. It didn't sound like it, judging from Detective Stanley's tone, but with the way our lives had been upending at every turn, we didn't know.

When we got there, Detective's Stanley and Cartwright, the woman who had questioned Tray, were both standing at the entrance waiting. Tray said she never told him her name when she was questioning him, but it was right there on her badge.

They took us to the same room this time.

Detective Stanley's face reddened. "Mia, Tray... It appears we owe you an apology."

My eyes narrowed. "For what?"

He cleared his throat, and Detective Cartwright remained silent, staring straight ahead like she wasn't in the room.

"Noland woke up last night. He is expected to make a full recovery, though he's still badly injured."

"Well, thank God for that. I take it he told you it wasn't us?"

Detective Stanley gave a short nod. "He did. Apparently, it was his cousin."

My jaw dropped as I turned to Tray in confusion. "His cousin?" I turned back to Detective Stanley. Life was getting so crazy. I could barely keep up.

So not only was Noland's ass crazy, his whole family was, too?

"Why would his cousin do that? Are we allowed to ask?" Tray said.

Detective Stanley nodded again. "Under normal circumstances, we wouldn't share that information, but since this was also a person who was a threat to you, Mia, we can share."

"A threat to me?" I was completely lost at this point.

Detective Stanley's next words cleared it all up for me. Apparently, Loryn, my ex best friend, was Noland's cousin. Detective Stanley didn't have all the details, but he shared that Noland revealed that Loryn had done this to him and that she was planning to come after me and Tray next.

"I knew that bitch was crazy!" Tray said as we were exiting the station for what we hoped to be the final time in our lives. The police ended up catching Loryn before they called us, so thankfully, she was already in custody. God only knew where her baby was.

Tray and I went to bring Tyriek for a surprise visit to Noland a few days later. He was going to be in the hospital for a few weeks, but he was well enough to sit up and have a conversation.

What he had to tell me and Tray was shocking, to say the least.

"Mia, I'm so sorry. I should have said something before," he said.

I kept calm because I was pissed that Noland knew who Loryn was the entire time I was confiding in him about what she had done to me, but said nothing.

He turned to Tray. "I apologize to you, too."

Tray looked confused, but he shrugged. "It's cool, man."

Noland licked his lips. I wondered why he wasn't reaching for Tyriek, but his next words told me why.

"Loryn told me Tyriek wasn't my son," he said. A tear came to his eyes.

"What do you mean?" I asked. "We got a DNA test."

He shook his head. "She had one of her homegirls that she knew at the office we sent them off to fake it for her. I guess her original plan was to try to fake both results, but they had already sent Tyrell's out before her friend could get it. She really made me believe Tyriek was mine."

He looked so hurt, I felt for him.

"Damn," Tray said.

"That's not all," Noland continued. "When she confessed what she did to me, I screamed on her. I told her I was gonna tell y'all what else she did, and I guess she just snapped."

"What else did she do?" I asked. Shit, at this point, anything was possible.

Noland turned to Tray. "You and Loryn never slept together."

Tray's eyes bulged. "What?"

Noland winced like a pain just shot through him, then he spilled the beans. "The night you were over her house, she slipped you a roofie. Her plan was to get you hard, then fuck you and get pregnant, but apparently she couldn't give you an erection."

"Oh my God..." I almost dropped my damn baby after hearing that.

Tyriek looked on like he was intrigued by the story. I covered his ears while balancing him in my lap. He couldn't understand us, anyway, I didn't think, but still.

"Are you serious?" Tray asked.

Noland nodded. "She called me over and asked me to do a favor. I didn't want to do it at first, but I was trying to help her out. I figured her plan to make you think you slept with her wouldn't work, anyway, so I helped her carry to you her bedroom. I had no idea she was already pregnant by another nigga. She had already stripped you by the time I got there, and I was disgusted, but I still helped put you in her bed."

"What the fuck, nigga?" Tray said, looking disgusted himself.

"After that I left, thinking it was over, but a few months later, here she was with another favor." Noland turned to me, and I already knew what he was going to say.

"She asked you to approach me," I said before he could speak.

He nodded. "But I swear, Mia. I really did have feelings for you. I think I fell in love."

I wiped a tear from my eye. "No, Noland, you fell into obsession. Thank you for almost ruining my fucking life."

I got up to leave, and Noland didn't bother to call out for me. Tray left with me.

Tray and I sent off for new DNA tests a week later, just to make sure, and Noland's story was confirmed. Tray was the father of both my babies.

I didn't hear from Noland after that, and I didn't care to, either.

Epilogue: Mia

After all the drama Tray and I went through, we wanted to take a vacation. The night before we left, however, my mom invited us over for dinner. Apparently, things were getting serious with her little boyfriend, so she wanted us to meet him.

I was happy for her since she'd barely dated anyone since my dad.

I got the shock of my life when I walked in to see Jeff sitting at the dining room table, his stick and guide dog right next to him.

"Jeff?" I asked when I picked my jaw up from the floor.

"Mia!" He said, his eyes twinkling. "I told you I'd met someone new."

I turned to my mom, half-curious, half-appalled. "Mom, ewww, why didn't you tell me? And how the heck did you meet Jeff?"

Jeff pretended to be offended. "What do you mean, ew? I am sexy as hell."

Tray burst out laughing at that one.

Mom looked a little embarrassed. "Mia, I swear I wanted to tell you, but Jeff said he wanted it to be a surprise. He told me all about your conversations with him at The Cafeteria."

"How did he figure out that you were my mother though?"

Jeff answered that. "Your voices are similar, and you have similar scents. Plus your mother went on and on about her daughter, Mia. I finally asked her to describe you a bit more, and she mentioned your boyfriend Tray. I asked her if you ever went to The Cafeteria, and she said you go there every day for lunch. That's how we figured it out. Small world, isn't it?"

All I could do was shake my head, looking back and forth between them. "I'm glad you two are happy."

Dinner was eventful, to say the least.

Six months later...

Thankfully, life was somewhat normal now, despite the fact that my two ex-best friends were both locked up. One in a psychiatric facility, and one in prison.

Tray and I finally got married, thank God. We decided to just go to the courthouse and have a small reception since I wouldn't have bridesmaids due to the fact that apparently, I wasn't the best at picking friends.

Noland shot me a congratulations comment when I posted our pictures. I had forgotten to block him and it must have slipped my mind since he never reached out again before then.

I peeked at his page and saw he had a new girlfriend, who was pregnant, judging from their professional maternity photos.

They looked cute together with her huge baby bump and their pink and white color-coordinated outfits.

It had been enough time since everything took place, so my anger had subsided.

I was happy for him.

Tray and I were doing great. I ended up quitting my job without giving notice to Evelin, and Tray ended up finishing school and getting a full-time job at the dentist's office he did his internship at.

Tyriek and Tyrell were starting to walk, and it was only a matter of time before they started running around and destroying everything in our house, as my mom said they would do.

I welcomed that idea. It was much better than the drama I'd experienced up to this point.

The End

Dear Reader,

I truly hope you enjoyed this story. If you did, please leave a rating or review to comment your thoughts on the book or characters.

Want to read another thriller? I have plenty more for you, all in different sub-genres.

Turn the page to explore.

Until next time,

Tanisha Stewart

The Maintenance Man: A Twisted Urban Love Triangle Thriller

"Momma said don't play with fire, 'cause one day, you might get burned..."

Malachi is a self-proclaimed ladies man; others would describe him as a dog. He sees women as disposable, despite the fact that he claims to be madly in love with his girlfriend, Zoe.

Everything appears to be going well for him, until the **bodies start dropping**.

Caught up in a race against time with too many suspects to figure out who's after him, it's time for Malachi to finally **come clean**. Is there a chance for Malachi's redemption?

Or is he just biding his time until his number is called?

Check it out here: <u>The Maintenance Man: A Twisted Urban Love Triangle Thriller</u>

Should Have Thought Twice: A Psychological Thriller

They say to always watch the quiet ones, because you never know when they might snap.

Shatina is a young woman with a troubled past and present. She lives in the shadows of her fraternal twin sister, who sucked up all the beauty genes, her best friend, whose seductive charm will sway any boy who listens, and her cousin, who is more than a knockout, but a force to be reckoned with.

Shatina feels like she has nothing going for her but her grades and her full scholarship to a four year institution of her choice... until someone comes along to threaten that.

Shatina has faced threats before, and little does anyone know, she has gained vindication over all of her enemies, one by one. Except this last one might be a bit more of a challenge than she bargained for.

Check it out here: <u>Should Have Thought Twice: A Psychological Thriller</u>

That's What You Get: An Urban Romance Thriller

We all do things that we live to regret, but when you harm the wrong ones, you get what you get.

Junior cheated. Marlena is furious. She resolves to teach him a lesson. What starts as a simple act of revenge, however, quickly takes a dangerous turn.

While Marlena was busy getting back at Junior, someone else happened to be planning a revenge of her own against Marlena. The deadly kind.

Marlena finds herself in a race against time to no longer change her man. Now she has to save him. And herself.

Check it out on Kindle Vella: [That's What You Get: An Urban Romance Thriller]

Caught Up With The 'Rona: An Urban Sci Fi Thriller

Cordell's luck could not be any worse. A young black man, a full-time student, doing his best to give back to his community by serving as a substitute teacher, only to receive an email which stated that his job would be suspended for the next three weeks due to the Coronavirus.

Frustrated about the situation, he vents to his lifelong friend, Jerone. Shortly after their conversation begins, they are approached by Markellis, a neighborhood hustler who always tries to sell Cordell and Jerone on his get-rich-quick schemes...

But this one is different. Cordell is pressed for cash, so he convinces Jerone to go along with Markellis' proposal.

No sooner than they say yes, Cordell and Jerone are swept up in an almost unspeakable conspiracy, with less than three weeks to turn it around...

Only it's much more than just Cordell and Jerone's lives that are at stake.

Check it out here: Caught Up With The 'Rona: An Urban Sci Fi Thriller

December 21st: An Urban Supernatural Suspense

Flick is a regular guy, living a regular life, then the night of Thanksgiving came.

It all started with a conversation he had with his cousin Bru that got a little heated.

Tensions rose, but things calmed down when he went to his mother's house for the family dinner.

Little did he know, that's when his life would begin to shift in a direction that he never expected.

December 21st, Saturn and Jupiter aligning, competing belief systems... what did it all mean?

Nothing, Flick thought.
Until the first event.
Then the second.

Follow Flick's journey in this Urban Supernatural Suspense as he tries to figure out exactly what's going on.

Is he losing his mind?

Or does everything that is happening have a deeper meaning?

Check it out here: December 21st: An Urban Supernatural Suspense

Tanisha Stewart's Books

Even Me Series
Even Me
Even Me, The Sequel
Even Me, Full Circle

When Things Go Series
When Things Go Left
When Things Get Real
When Things Go Right

For My Good Series
For My Good: The Prequel
For My Good: My Baby Daddy Ain't Ish
For My Good: I Waited, He Cheated
For My Good: Torn Between The Two
For My Good: You Broke My Trust
For My Good: Better or Worse
For My Good: Love and Respect
Rick and Sharmeka: A BWWM Romance

Betrayed Series
Betrayed By My So-Called Friend
Betrayed By My So-Called Friend, Part 2
Betrayed 3: Camaiyah's Redemption
Betrayed Series: Special Edition

Phate Series
Phate: An Enemies to Lovers Romance
Phate 2: An Enemies to Lovers Romance
Leisha & Manuel: Love After Pain

The Real Ones Series
Find You A Real One: A Friends to Lovers Romance
Find You A Real One 2: A Friends to Lovers Romance
Janie & E: Life Lessons

Standalones
A Husband, A Boyfriend, & a Side Dude
In Love With My Uber Driver
You Left Me At The Altar
Where. Is. Haseem?! A Romantic-Suspense Comedy
Caught Up With The 'Rona: An Urban Sci-Fi Thriller
#DOLO: An Awkward, Non-Romantic Journey Through Singlehood
December 21st: An Urban Supernatural Suspense
Should Have Thought Twice: A Psychological Thriller
Everybody Ain't Your Friend
The Maintenance Man

Made in the USA
Las Vegas, NV
20 August 2021

28561469R00134